GILDED GIRL

PAMELA KELLEY

The letter that changed everything arrived on a cold, dreary Monday. Eliza Chapman was arranging Lady Caroline Ashton's hair into a French twist when her father, Lord Ashton, knocked at the door of her dressing room. The door was half-open, but he knocked anyway.

"You look lovely. Your mother's pearls suit you."

Lady Caroline was getting ready for an important dinner party. She was twenty, two years younger than Eliza, and her family was anxious for her to meet someone appropriate.

"Lord Billings is going to be swept off his feet by you. He'd make a very good match, you know," her father added.

Lady Caroline sighed. "Yes, you keep telling me that." She turned and smiled at him a moment later, though. "I'll be on my best behavior. Promise."

Her father laughed. Eliza had always admired the bond

between the two. Lord Ashton clearly thought the world of his daughter. And she adored him, too. Eliza was a bit envious of that. Not their station in life, she knew better than to wish for something that she had no control over, but she longed for that kind of closeness. She'd had it once, with her mother, until she recently passed. But she never knew her father.

While the two of them talked, Eliza let her mind drift, and it went as it often did to her last moments with her mother. She'd been so sick and yet she struggled to tell Eliza something. But all she'd managed to say was, "I need to tell you the truth about your father."

She wasn't able to get the explanation out, though. Her energy was fading and her last two words were mumbled and almost incoherent. "A letter." Eliza had no idea what that meant. Did she send a letter? Receive one? What was in the letter? Eliza didn't know if she'd ever find out.

"Eliza?" By Lady Caroline's suddenly sharp tone, Eliza guessed it wasn't the first time she'd called her name.

"Yes?"

"Stop daydreaming! Father was trying to get your attention."

"I'm sorry, what is it?"

Lord Ashton spoke. "Lady Ashton would like to see you in her study at your earliest convenience."

Eliza secured Lady Caroline's hair with a final pin and took a step back.

Lady Caroline turned her head to admire her hair in all

directions before nodding and saying, "That will do. You can run along."

Eliza scurried out of the room and down the long hallway and two flights of stairs until she reached the study. She knocked lightly on the closed door.

"You may enter."

Eliza pushed the door open and stepped inside. Lady Ashton sat behind a large, gleaming mahogany desk. She had a stack of papers in front of her and a newly opened envelope and folded letter on top.

"Have a seat."

Eliza sat in one of the two leather padded chairs directly across from the desk and waited. The only other time she'd been sent to the study, she'd been in trouble for not following a rule she wasn't aware of. She wondered what she'd done this time.

"Do you have any idea why you are here?"

"No. I am sorry, though, for whatever I did."

Lady Ashton smiled. "You're not in trouble, my dear. This is highly unusual, though. I've just received a letter... From your father."

Eliza leaned forward in her chair. Surely, she'd heard wrong. "My father?"

"You don't know anything about this?" She looked intrigued. "Do you even know who your father is?"

"My mother never said. She tried to tell me, before she passed, but she couldn't manage it."

"I see." Lady Ashton fiddled with the letter for a

moment as though debating what to do, what to say. "Maybe it's best if I just read this to you."

Eliza nodded and waited for her to begin.

"My dearest Lady Ashton, it has recently come to my attention that I may have a third daughter. I believe Eliza Chapman is currently in your employ as a ladies' maid. I met her mother many years ago when you and Lord Ashton were kind enough to invite my family to spend several weeks with you one summer. Vivian and I grew close, but we lost touch when I returned to the states. I never knew that we had a daughter together until she sent me a letter. She mentioned being sick and wanting me to know before she passed.

After much consideration, I would like to invite Eliza to come to New York City to meet her family. I want to try to be a father to her, if she'll allow it. I've enclosed a one-way ticket for her passage. Please give her my best regards and let her know that my daughters Alice and Rose also look forward to meeting her. I've enclosed a small sum of money so that she can purchase whatever she may need for the trip. Thank you for your kind assistance in this matter and I do apologize for stealing away one of your ladies' maids. Yours most sincerely, Ward Redfield."

Lady Ashton stopped reading and looked up for Eliza's response, but she was speechless.

"Do you recognize the name Ward Redfield?" Lady Ashton asked.

"I don't. Should I?"

"He is one of the richest and most successful men in

Manhattan. His Upper East Side mansion is the largest in the city. Your father is a very rich man."

It was a lot to absorb. "And he wants me to come visit?"

"He sent a one-way ticket. He wants you to stay. To go home."

"Home. To New York City." Eliza was stunned.

Lady Ashton leaned back in her chair and met Eliza's gaze. "It won't be easy, you know. There is the small matter of being illegitimate. Americans may be more accepting of that than we are, but it may still be problematic for you. It would be impossible here. But, perhaps we can help. Ward Redfield is a very good friend."

Eliza thought about what it all meant. This man had met her mother years ago, left her with child and went home, having no idea.

"I wonder why she never told him?" What would have happened if her mother had sent the letter when she first found out?

Lady Ashton shook her head sadly. "It simply wasn't done. She might not have been believed and even if she was, his parents never would have allowed them to be together. We always wondered what happened with your mother, who she was involved with. She never said a word to anyone. And we never judged."

Eliza nodded. She knew her mother was always grateful that the Ashtons had kept her on when they learned of the pregnancy and that they didn't ask any questions. Like Eliza, her mother had been a ladies' maid too, for Lady Ashton.

Lady Ashton picked up her bell and rang it twice. A moment later, one of the housemaids stepped into the room.

"You rang, m'lady?"

"Yes, could you please fetch Lady Caroline and tell her to hurry?"

Minutes later, Lady Caroline strolled into the room, looking annoyed. "What is so important that I had to rush down here?"

"I think you should sit."

Lady Caroline sat in the chair next to Eliza and listened as her mother explained what was in the letter. When she finished, Lady Caroline's first words were, "So, this means I'm losing my ladies' maid?"

Lady Ashton nodded. "That is correct. Though you won't go without. Mrs. Thompson will send another girl up to take Eliza's place." She looked at her daughter thoughtfully for a moment before adding, "You and Eliza are about the same size. Take her to your room and choose a selection of your dresses, enough to fill two trunks. She'll need daytime, evening and special occasion."

Lady Caroline's jaw dropped in confusion. "You want me to give her my clothes?"

"Yes, dear. You have plenty that you've worn and have no intention of wearing again. You know you never repeat your gowns that you've worn in public. They're just going to collect dust. This will tide Eliza over until she reaches New York and can do more shopping."

"More shopping?" Eliza felt dazed.

Lady Ashton smiled, a gleam of mischief in her eyes. "Eliza, you have no idea how your life is going to change." She glanced at her daughter. "Caroline, I'll have Mrs. Thompson send one of the footmen up with the trunks. Now, off with you both. Caroline, I hope you'll be excited for Eliza. Make sure you pick out some of your prettiest dresses."

Lady Caroline looked almost as dazed as Eliza, but finally managed a smile.

"All right, Eliza. Let's go shopping."

"Eliza, I'll have Mrs. Thompson see you about coordinating your departure. Until then, please keep this to yourself. It's best if the rest of the staff don't know your business. As this is highly unusual."

Eliza nodded. "Of course." She guessed that she still had several weeks before she'd be leaving. It would be hard to keep the news to herself, but she imagined that Lady Ashton didn't want the news to upset the staff or to give them ideas that they could aspire to rise above their station, too.

Once they reached her suite, Lady Caroline's mood improved, and she actually seemed excited for Eliza.

"Mother is right. We are about the same size, though you are a bit slimmer around the waist and a little fuller on top. I think most of my dresses should fit you well enough. I have to admit, I'm a bit jealous."

"Jealous? Of me?" Eliza couldn't imagine why.

"Yes, silly. You're going to the United States. To New York City. I've never been, and it's supposed to be wonderful. My mother is right, you're very lucky. This is an incredible opportunity for you. This doesn't happen to most people—the chance to enter a new world. Are you excited?"

"Yes. Stunned is more like it, but yes, I'm excited to meet my father and my sisters."

"Right. Two sisters. That will be interesting for you." She turned and flung open the doors to her huge walk-in closet. "Well, shall we pick out some dresses?"

They spent the next hour going through Lady Caroline's sizable wardrobe and selecting a wide range of dresses and hats that would suit just about every occasion. The clothes had barely been worn. Some, like her fanciest ball gowns, had only been worn once. Eliza gasped and sighed with happiness as Lady Caroline handed Eliza a dress she'd fallen in love with almost a year ago. It was a beautiful, shimmering blue ball gown and Eliza thought it looked fit for a princess. To think that now it would be hers! And that she might have an opportunity to wear it. She almost pinched herself in disbelief.

Mrs. Thompson stopped by looking for Eliza as they finished selecting the final dress. Eliza liked Mrs. Thompson. She oversaw housekeeping and the kitchen, and Eliza had known her for as long as she could remember. Mrs. Thompson looked around the room at the piles of clothing.

"Henry and James will be in shortly with the trunks for you. Go ahead and pack carefully and then they'll take them down to the carriage house for loading. You'll be leaving Thursday morning at five am. Your ship leaves at eight."

Eliza must have heard incorrectly.

"This Thursday?" It was just two days away. She couldn't possibly be leaving so soon. She wasn't ready. She thought she'd have a few weeks to get used to the idea.

Mrs. Thompson smiled. "Yes, dear. Lady Ashton called to confirm and you're all set. Remember, not a word to the others."

"Yes, of course."

"Eliza, you will be missed. But, I couldn't be happier for you. Your mother is up there, looking down on us, and I know she's thrilled too."

"Thank you."

"Well, I have to run down to dinner," Lady Caroline said. "Eliza, you can manage packing up the rest by yourself?"

Eliza nodded. "Yes, and thank you. I'm so very grateful. You and Lady Ashton have been so generous."

Lady Caroline smiled. "I'm glad to see they will get another life. I've always thought it was silly we only wear some of these dresses once."

She and Mrs. Thompson left together and Eliza quickly got to work, packing all the dresses efficiently in the two trunks that James and Henry brought to the room. She filled each of them to the brim, added the hats, and carefully closed the lid.

* * *

Eliza went downstairs to the kitchen and the servants'

dining room, where the evening meal was being plated as she arrived. It was a smaller group than usual, as there was a dinner party for twenty going on upstairs and half a dozen or so footmen were serving.

"Gravy, Eliza?" Mrs. Wiggins, the main cook, asked.

"Yes, please." Eliza took the plate of roasted chicken, bread stuffing and potatoes, all covered with gravy and a few green beans on the side. She went into the dining room and sat next to her best friend, and fellow ladies' maid, Sophie.

"Someone's going on a trip," Sophie said immediately.

"Oh?"

"Henry said there was a call for two trunks to be brought to Lady Caroline's room. I wonder where she's going. Has she said anything to you?"

Eliza had to force herself not to smile. "No, she hasn't said a thing. Maybe it's not her?"

"Who else could it be if the trunks were sent to her room? I wonder where she is going?"

"I have no idea." Eliza was tempted to confide in Sophie, but she was the worst secret keeper. Sophie wouldn't be able to resist telling everyone. And Eliza had given her word not to say anything.

The next day was a strange one, as Eliza went about her daily routine, same as usual, yet it was the last day she was going to be working as a ladies' maid. Although she found that hard to believe and was fully prepared to have to look for work again. Perhaps her father's family only meant for her to visit? What if they didn't like her? Maybe she would stay and try to find work in New York City if she needed to. She was excited about all the possibilities that were ahead of her. And a little scared too, but mostly excited.

Lady Caroline wished her well at the end of the day. "I will miss you. It's strange to think you won't be here anymore. I am feeling a bit sorry for myself," she admitted. "But I'm more excited for you. Please write to me once you are settled and let me know how you are getting on?"

"I will, I promise."

Mrs. Thompson called for her to come by her office before dinner. When Eliza stepped into the room, Mrs. Thompson was sitting at her desk, writing a letter. She stood when she saw Eliza.

"I just wanted to say a proper goodbye, my dear. And to wish you all good things and a safe journey to your new life. I'm so very happy for you." She pulled her in for a hug and squeezed her tight before letting go and dabbing at her eyes.

"Thank you. I'll miss you too. I'll write once I'm settled."

"Wonderful, I look forward to it."

At dinner, Sophie cocked her head and looked at Eliza curiously. "You know something, don't you? And you're not saying. I can tell. You're being very quiet and mysterious. You must spill. You know I won't say anything."

Eliza laughed. "You know you can't help yourself."

"Well, true. But tell me anyway. Where is Lady Caroline going?"

"She's not going anywhere. I swear, that's the truth."

Sophie sighed. "How strange. Must be someone else then."

"Must be. Or maybe she was just donating some old clothes? That would explain the trunks, possibly."

"Oh, I suppose so. That's not nearly as exciting, though."

"No, I guess not. So, have you heard anything about Henry and Ava?" There was a rumor going around that the footman and the ladies' maid had started a romance.

Sophie leaned forward and lowered her voice. "Well, both deny it, of course. But, I don't believe them. I've seen the way they look at each other. What do you think?"

"Hard to say. You never really know what people are up to."

2

*T*hursday morning at a quarter to five, Eliza quietly walked downstairs to the carriage house. She carried one bag, which held all the money she had in the world, including what her father had sent along with the ticket—one book, two apples, a small hand mirror and a brush. She was wearing one of the gifted dresses that Lady Caroline had declared would be most suitable for traveling.

Brian, the Ashtons' main driver, raised his eyes when he saw Eliza, but said nothing other than hello as he opened the door for her to settle inside the carriage. He loaded the trunks in the back and, after a moment, they were on their way.

The journey to Liverpool took two hours. They arrived at the docking pier at a few minutes past seven. Brian lifted Eliza's two heavy trunks out of the back of the carriage and waved down a ship's porter to take them. He'd been silent the whole trip, but Eliza had noticed his curious glances now and then. As she turned to say goodbye, he finally spoke.

"I'm sworn to total secrecy, you know. No one can know you left with two trunks full of Lady Caroline's clothing. I don't know where you are going, but I suspect you have quite an adventure ahead of you. I wish you well."

Eliza grinned. "Thank you, Brian." She didn't know him well, but knew he was regarded as someone who could be trusted. She sensed that her secret was safe with him.

She followed the porter that took her trunks and entered the main reservations and check-in area and waited in line. When she handed over her ticket, the woman behind the desk smiled.

"Ms. Chapman, the porter is bringing your luggage to your stateroom. You are in the first-first-class suite 7B. We will be boarding shortly. Have a pleasant journey."

Eliza hadn't even considered that she might be in first-class. She'd never traveled anywhere before, but knew there were different levels of staterooms and assumed she'd be with the majority in the more modest ones. When they were called to board and she opened the door to her room, she almost dropped her bag. Her stateroom was a large suite, elegantly appointed with plush carpeting, rich velvet drapes and a sitting area that was bigger than she'd imagined the entire room would be.

Her trunks were waiting for her and once she was past the shock of the luxurious room, Eliza began unpacking and withdrew the dresses that Lady Caroline had chosen for her week on the ship. She knew there would be formal dinners and that she would be assigned a table where she would eat with the same people each night. She was a bit nervous about that and hoped that she wouldn't be asked too many questions.

Lady Caroline had suggested that if she was asked for details, she could truthfully say that she'd been living abroad for the past year with the Ashtons and that she was going to be staying in Manhattan. And they came up with the perfect way for Eliza to explain her relationship to Wade Redfield, because saying she was his illegitimate daughter was unacceptable. Eliza just hoped she'd remember and get the details right when she was asked.

The ship got underway almost an hour later once everyone was aboard. Eliza spent the rest of the day settling in and unpacking before setting out and exploring. The ship was massive, bigger than she ever imagined, and there were so many people. The first-class section was quiet and calm compared to the rest of the ship. It was all lovely, but first-class was special. It had its own library, and there were a few books that Eliza had her eye on. She knew that she'd be spending quite a bit of time in the reading and writing room adjacent to the library. It was a luxury to be able to just relax and read for a whole week.

She had nothing to compare it to, but she was surprised nonetheless by the elegance of the first-class common area. It reminded her of an elegant hotel in London that she'd once traveled to with the Ashtons. She and another ladies' maid had shared a room, and they'd been amazed by the luxurious surroundings.

It was just as lovely in the ship's first-class area with its rich fabrics and beautiful furniture. And everyone she saw as she walked around was dressed grandly. She imagined many of her fellow passengers in first-class were titled. Eliza felt a bit like an imposter, as though she really shouldn't be there and might be asked to leave at any moment. She had to keep reminding herself that for the first time she actually did belong.

Eliza wasn't hungry enough or brave enough to venture to the dining room alone at noon. She thought it might be easier to make her first appearance later that evening for dinner, which was at seven. She had her table assignment, which was given to her when she boarded. Until then, she decided to read for a bit in her room and when she finally grew hungry later that afternoon, she ate one of the two apples she'd brought with her.

She managed to squeeze in a short nap too. The long day had caught up with her and she'd barely slept the night before, as she was worried about oversleeping for her early departure. She woke a little before six and set about getting ready for dinner, washing up and then staring at Lady Caroline's dresses, trying to decide which one to wear. She finally settled on a midnight blue silk evening gown that was flattering without hugging her curves too tightly. She'd be able to relax and indulge. Lady Caroline and her parents had traveled to New Zealand a few summers ago on one of the White Star ships and she'd told Eliza all about it when she returned. And she reminded Eliza about it when they were choosing her dresses.

"You don't want anything that is at all tight around the waist for dinner. Trust me on that."

So, even though Eliza knew what to expect, experiencing a ten-course meal was something else entirely. The food kept coming, and it was all delicious. They started with caviar and oysters with finely diced tomatoes and fresh herbs, followed by a delicate veal consommé topped with a single, sliced sea scallop, then poached salmon in a creamy butter sauce, followed by foie gras, tenderloin in a brandy butter sauce, sliced lamb, fragrant truffles over roasted asparagus, and finally, dessert, a rich chocolate mousse. She was really much too full for it, but somehow managed to take a few bites.

She was grateful for Lady Caroline's warning about the size and decadence of the dinner. Because her dress was so comfortable, she indulged more than she would have and half-way through the dinner, wondered how she could possibly eat more. But she did. They all did. She was seated at a table with five others and was also grateful for the many courses because it meant there was always something new to focus their attention on. The waiters were constantly adding and removing dishes from the table and pouring more wine. There was a different wine poured for each course, and they started the evening with a round of cocktails.

Eliza rarely drank alcohol. She typically had a glass of champagne with the rest of the staff on New Year's Eve and the occasional glass of wine on other holidays. She'd never had a cocktail before and wasn't sure what to order, but she followed the lead of the woman sitting next to her, who ordered a Manhattan straight up. She introduced herself as Duchess Grace Archibald, wife of Duke William Archibald, and her son, Lord Nick, who appeared to be around Eliza's age, maybe a few years older. The two men were both drinking Tom Collins cocktails. The other two ladies at the table were sisters, Mary and Ethel Robinson, and they were also drinking Manhattans. They were in their seventies and were visiting New York for the first time as well.

"We're both widows," Mary explained. "I lost my Tim ten years ago, but Ethel just lost her Ben nine months ago. We've always wanted to travel, so here we are."

"Tell us about yourself, dear," Grace asked as she reached for a sip of her cocktail and glanced at Eliza. "How does a lovely young woman happen to be traveling alone?"

Eliza took a deep breath and smiled, hoping that she would remember what she'd been studying to say. "I've been visiting friends abroad this past year, Lord and Lady Ashton."

Grace nodded, "I haven't met them, but do know who they are."

"My cousins in Manhattan invited me to visit. Perhaps you know them? My uncle is Ward Redfield."

That got the attention of William and Nick. William cleared his throat. "Did you say your uncle is Ward Redfield?"

Eliza nodded. "Yes. That's where I'm heading."

"We know Ward. He's a very successful businessman, your uncle. But you know that."

"Yes. I don't know much about the details of his business, though," she admitted, knowing that she wouldn't be expected to.

The Duchess smiled. "I'm sure our paths will cross again in Manhattan. We've been to several lovely parties at your uncle's home. We enjoy Manhattan and spend several months there each year."

Eliza couldn't help but notice that The Duchess showed more interest in her once she mentioned her uncle.

"There's a lecture tomorrow afternoon in the library—an author will be speaking about his book. I am planning to attend. Perhaps you'd like to join me?" The Duchess smiled as reached for her cocktail.

"I'd love that, actually. I did some exploring earlier and was planning to spend some time in the library."

"I will not be joining you ladies tomorrow," Nick said. "But perhaps I could interest Eliza in a dance later this evening?"

"A dance?" Eliza wasn't sure what he was referring to. The Duchess jumped in to explain.

"After dinner, there's music and dancing in the grand ballroom. We're all heading there shortly. You must join us," she insisted.

Eliza smiled. "Thank you. That sounds lovely."

And it was. Eliza was so full that her eyes were feeling heavy by the time they took their last bites, so walking around felt good and woke her up a bit as they made their way to the ballroom.

Nick ordered another round of cocktails for the table once they were seated and Eliza would have declined as she didn't know where she'd put it, but before she could say a word, the server was off to fill their order. She barely touched her drink, just taking the tiniest of sips now and then. But no one seemed to notice or care as they were all up dancing and it was fun to dance with Nick. He was a good partner and ignored that Eliza occasionally tripped over her feet. To say her dancing skills were lacking was an understatement. She'd typically danced once a year at the house staff Christmas party, which was always fun, but she knew she was rusty and was self-conscious about it.

"My cousin was often sick this year, and we didn't attend as many events as usual. I've missed dancing," she said. At least the last part of what she said was true. She'd often stop and watch Lady Caroline whirling around the ballroom in the arms of one of her many handsome suitors. The Ashtons loved to throw lavish dinner parties and balls with music and dancing.

"I think you're quite the elegant dancer." He grinned. "We'll just have to stay out here so you can make up for lost time. I'll show you what you've missed this past year. I've learned a few things."

Eliza laughed. "I appreciate that, and I'm ready to learn. Show me the way."

Much later, when they were both winded from laughing and dancing for so long, they took a break and decided to walk outside for some fresh air. They stood on one of the long decks and leaned against the railing. It was dark, but Eliza could still see the sea below and smell the salt in the air.

"So, you're going to be staying with your uncle. What are your plans while you're here?" Nick asked. "Is it a short visit, or will you be in the city for a while?"

"I don't have any particular plans yet." Eliza thought for a moment. She really didn't know what she would be doing, but she made an educated guess. "The usual things I suppose, parties, dinners and I'd love to visit the Metropolitan Museum of Art. I'm not sure how long I'll be staying, but I don't have plans to leave in the near future."

"I'm sure I'll see you at some of the parties. You tend to see the same faces at those gatherings. I haven't been to that museum yet. Perhaps we should explore it together?" He smiled and Eliza was dazzled by the pair of dimples that gave his very handsome face a mischievous look. He was flirting with her! And Eliza was fascinated because no one had ever flirted with her before. She couldn't help wondering, though, if he'd be paying her this much attention if she hadn't mentioned her uncle's name.

Although his mother was a duchess, so it was more than likely that they were equally successful and wealthy. Not that Eliza cared about that. But she was curious about them.

"What brings your family to Manhattan? Is yours a short stay or will you also be staying a while?"

"My mother loves Manhattan. For the past few years,

we've split our time each year and spend about six months in the states. So, I'm sure our paths will cross often. Have you been there before?"

Eliza shook her head. "No, it's my first time, actually."

"Oh, how marvelous. Well, you are in for a treat. And perhaps you'll need someone to show you around the city a bit."

Eliza smiled. "That would be lovely. It's such a big city that I wasn't sure where to start. Though I'm sure my cousins have some plans for me as well." She wasn't at all sure of that, but she hoped it was true.

"I've met Alice and Rose. I'm sure they have something in mind for you. Are you close with them?" His expression was hard to read, and she wondered how well he knew her cousins. She wanted to ask him about them, but knew that would lead to more questions.

"I hope to be. It's been years since I've seen them."

"When you see them, be sure to give them my regards."

"I will."

3

*T*he rest of the week flew by in a happy blur. One day rolled into the next and was a whirlwind of dinners and lectures and more music and dancing. Eliza enjoyed the company of the three women, especially the two older ladies, who loved to read as much as Eliza did, while The Duchess seemed somewhat bored by it all.

And Eliza had a fun time with Nick. He was charming, and they danced every night. By the end of the week, she was feeling more confident about her dance skills and nervously looking forward to parties or balls that she might be invited to in the city. She supposed it depended on how she got along with her new sisters and if they chose to include her. She hoped that they would welcome her. She was excited to meet them. She'd always wanted siblings.

The last evening aboard the ship was bittersweet as their little group had grown close and it felt like they were on a vacation that was about to end. At least that's what Eliza imagined a vacation might be like. She'd never actually had one. She'd taken time off but never was able to go anywhere. When the ship entered New York Harbor, Eliza, along with many passengers, stood on an outside deck and felt a sense of wonder as they glided by the Statue of Liberty. She was about to enter a whole new world.

"Someone is coming to meet you?" The Duchess asked as they disembarked the ship.

"Yes, I was told that someone would be waiting for me." Lady Ashton had told her it would probably be one of their servants, most likely their driver.

"Very good. We'll see you soon, my dear. Please give our best regards to your uncle."

"And I'll be in touch soon for our first tour," Nick promised.

Eliza watched them go with a fleeting sense of panic that she quickly willed away. There was nothing to be nervous about. She should just feel excited. However, chasing her nerves away was easier said than done. One of the first-class porters spotted her and wheeled her luggage over.

"Where would you like this to go, miss?"

Eliza looked around, searching for someone holding a card with her name. She didn't see anyone, but the area was very crowded.

"There's someone coming. He should be here any moment." She scanned the area again and this time, she saw him. A man who looked to be just a few years older than her, wearing a long black coat and matching hat and holding a white sign with her name handwritten in black ink.

"There he is!" The porter followed her and as she got closer, she waved to the man holding the sign and looking around. He broke into a relieved grin when he saw her.

"Eliza Chapman?"

"Yes!"

"I'm Harry. Harry Ford, the Redfield family's driver." He grabbed her bags and the two trunks from the porter and put them in the back of the carriage. Once they were set, he came around and helped Eliza into the passenger side of the carriage and soon they were on their way.

"Have you worked for the family long?" Eliza asked as they drove off. She was fascinated by the hustle and bustle of the city, with so many people walking around, and horses and carriages gliding by.

"Eight years. I started with them when I was eighteen and took over as the main driver two years ago."

"Do you enjoy working for them?" Eliza was curious to know more about her father and his family.

He nodded. "I do. They've been good to me. I'm not looking to be a driver forever, though. I have a plan."

He sat taller in his seat, and Eliza found herself curious to know more.

"What is your plan?"

He grinned. "I'm going into retail. I want to open a shop that will have everything people could possibly want."

"Like a general store? That's a good idea."

"Bigger than that. A department store." He sat up taller in his seat and she saw determination and excitement in his eyes.

"What is a department store?"

"It's a big store that has everything you could ever want. I won't be able to start out as big as Macy's, but someday, that's the goal. I'll have a clothing shop first, fine men's and women's clothing, shoes and accessories."

"That sounds impressive. How will you do that? Do you know anything about running a store?"

"I know a fair bit about the retail trade, mostly from the supplier side. My father, before he died, had a business making clothing. He used the best fabrics, and was known for his quality."

Eliza wondered why he wasn't working in the family business, but felt it was rude to ask. She didn't have to wait long, though, before Harry volunteered the information.

"My father passed suddenly, almost ten years ago. We didn't realize it, but he'd fallen behind with paying his suppliers and the business went under. But someday, when I've saved enough money, I'm going to start my business and I'll make him proud."

Eliza smiled. His enthusiasm was contagious. "I bet you will."

Harry turned onto Fifth Avenue and Eliza gasped at the beauty of the mansions that lined the street. Harry grinned. "They call this stretch Millionaire's Row." He pointed out some of the grandest residences, "That's where the Vander-bilts live and that one is the Astor's." He slowed and pulled up to a residence that was even more grand. "And here we are."

She'd anticipated that her father's home would be similar in size to the one she'd lived in all her life, but this was double or maybe even triple the size. It was exhilarating and intimidating at the same time. She took a deep breath.

"It's been so long since I've seen them," she lied. Hoping to explain her nervousness.

"None of them are home at the moment. They should all be back later this evening. I was told to bring you in to meet Mrs. Smith, the head housekeeper. She'll get you settled. Follow me." He jumped out of the carriage and tied the reins to a post. Eliza followed him along a cobblestone path to the front entrance, where Harry paused and then knocked on the door.

It was opened a moment later by a young man in black servant's attire. Eliza guessed that he might be a footman. He nodded when he saw Harry.

Harry held the door open so Eliza could step inside. "Daniel, could you please let Mrs. Smith know that Miss Chapman has arrived?"

The young man turned to scurry off and almost bumped into a woman who looked to be in her mid-fifties. She wore a dark gray dress with black boots and a black shawl. She smiled as she approached them.

"I'll take it from here, Harry. Could you please bring Miss Chapman's luggage to the blue room?"

"Of course." Harry glanced at Eliza and smiled. "Miss

Chapman, it was a pleasure to meet you. Enjoy the rest of your day." She watched him go and shivered as the cool air rushed in when he opened the front door. She turned her attention back to the woman standing before her.

"As you may have gathered, I am Mrs. Smith. I am the head housekeeper here and oversee the staff and manage the home. Your uncle has been looking forward to your visit. He and the girls are visiting his sister, who has been sick. They should all be home in time for the evening meal."

"Oh. Thank you. It's lovely to meet you." Eliza wondered how she was to entertain herself for the rest of the day.

"If you follow me, I'll show you to your room. I'm sure you'll be wanting to rest after your long journey." Mrs. Smith turned and Eliza followed her down the long hall and to a set of richly carpeted stairs. Mrs. Smith was somewhat formal, more business-like than friendly, as they walked up the stairs. But Eliza was curious and attempted to converse. "Have you worked for the family long?"

"It will be thirty years this month," she said proudly.

When they reached the second floor, they walked down a long hallway before stepping into a bedroom suite. There were two rooms and they were lovely—a large bedroom and a connecting sitting room. The walls were covered in a rich, shimmery blue fabric and the bedding was a similar shade of blue and the drapes at the windows, too. It was clear why it was referred to as the blue room.

Mrs. Smith opened the drapes on the two main

windows, letting in the light. Eliza guessed that the room hadn't been used in some time. She stepped toward the window and looked at the view below. It overlooked Fifth Avenue and she could see elegantly dressed men and women walking along the street and carriages going by.

"I trust you'll be comfortable here?" Mrs. Smith said.

"Oh, I'm sure I will be. It's lovely."

"Dinner is at eight. I'll have some refreshments brought up in an hour or so that should tide you over until then. I'll also send Miriam, your maid, up and you can let her know when you'd like her to draw a bath."

A maid! It was surreal to think that she'd gone from being a ladies' maid to having one. "Thank you."

"Ah, there's Harry with your luggage." Mrs. Smith turned at the sound of footsteps. Harry and Daniel entered the room, each carrying one of her large trunks. They set them down, nodded at Eliza and Mrs. Smith, and went on their way.

"Miriam can help you unpack as well. If there's anything else you need. Just ring the bell." She showed Eliza where the bell system was in the room, which would ring downstairs to summon assistance. She took a step toward the door. "It was a pleasure to meet you, Miss Chapman. I hope you will be comfortable here."

"Thank you."

4

*E*liza had every intention of opening her trunks and starting to unpack, but she decided to sit down first and rest on her bed for just a moment. The next thing she knew, there was a soft knock on the door. She thought that she'd closed her eyes for just a moment, but a quick glance at the clock on the wall showed that over an hour had passed.

She sat up and called for whoever had knocked on the door to come in. The nap had done her good, and she felt refreshed and ready to tackle the unpacking. The door opened slowly and a slight young woman with a pile of unruly strawberry curls tucked under a crisp white hat stepped timidly into the room.

"I hope I'm not disturbing you, miss?"

Eliza smiled. "No, not at all. I just had a quick nap."

The girl nodded. "My name is Miriam and I'll be attending to you. I've brought you a sandwich and some hot tea. Mrs. Smith suggested that I might want to help you unpack as well."

Miriam set the tray of food on the small table by the window. And waited for further instruction.

When Mrs. Smith had mentioned having some food sent up earlier, Eliza didn't think anything of it, but now she appreciated the gesture as her stomach was grumbling.

"Thank you so much. That looks wonderful. I would welcome your help actually as there are quite a lot of clothes to unpack and you might know best about where to put everything."

The young girl smiled. "I'm happy to help, miss. Why don't you sit and enjoy your meal, and I'll get started."

Eliza made her way to the small table and once she was settled, she took a sip of the hot tea and a tentative bite of the sandwich. It was good bread, and the sliced turkey was still warm and delicious. It didn't take her long to finish. While she ate, Miriam opened the trunks and began taking out dress after dress and hanging them in a large closet off the sitting room.

When Eliza finished her meal, she jumped up and began to help Miriam. The two women worked quickly, and it didn't take long to get everything out of the trunks and into the closet. When they finished, Miriam turned to Eliza and asked, "would you like me to draw you a bath?"

"Yes, please. That would be marvelous." After the long trip and formal dinner ahead, Eliza welcomed the opportunity to freshen up and look her best for the dinner.

Miriam went to draw her a bath and let Eliza know

when it was ready. "Shall I come back in an hour to help you dress and get ready for dinner?"

"Yes, please. Thank you." It still seemed so strange to Eliza to have someone to attend to her needs instead of being the one helping someone else get ready for dinner. She eased herself into the tub. The hot water felt wonderful, and she soaked in the water until her skin was all wrinkly. When she finally emerged from the bath, she saw that Miriam had laid a bathrobe on her bed. She dried off and slipped into the bathrobe. As she combed out her long hair, she tried to quell the butterflies that danced in her stomach as she thought about meeting her father and sisters for the first time at dinner.

Miriam returned as promised and helped Eliza to choose the perfect dress for dinner. She wasn't sure how formal the attire would be.

"They do dress for dinner every evening," Miriam told her. "You have a lovely selection of dresses—any of these would do nicely." She pointed out five dresses that were all grander than Eliza had imagined would be appropriate. She was surprised to see how formally they dressed for dinner in America. And she was so grateful that Lady Ashton had insisted she take so many of Lady Caroline's dresses. It would've been quite embarrassing otherwise.

Once Eliza was dressed, Miriam arranged her hair in an elegant French twist.

She held up a hand mirror so Eliza could see how beautiful the twist looked.

"Oh, thank you, Miriam. You did a wonderful job."

She looked pleased by the compliment. "You look lovely, miss."

"Please, call me Eliza."

Miriam looked conflicted and after a long moment, she nodded and said, "very well, miss Eliza."

Eliza smiled. She understood that as a servant, Miriam didn't feel comfortable calling her only by her first name.

"The family usually gathers in the drawing room by 7:45 if you would like to go down to meet them."

Like heading into the lions' den. The thought of heading down alone to meet her new family was a bit terrifying. But Eliza tried to reassure herself that it would be fine. Her father had invited her here, after all. She hoped that her sisters would be happy to make her acquaintance, as well.

She still had about a half hour before it would be time to head downstairs. Miriam left and promised to return later that evening to help her get ready for bed.

Eliza found her book and sat back down at the small table by the window to read for a bit. It was hard to focus on the story though, as her stomach was still a mess of nerves. She kept glancing out the window at the carriages going by, wondering if any of them would turn into the driveway. But none did. Or if they did, she missed it. She guessed that her family had arrived some time ago, probably while she was sleeping.

She kept glancing at the clock incessantly and finally, when it was almost a quarter to eight, she closed her book and stood. She checked her appearance one final time before slowly making her way downstairs. Miriam had forgotten to tell her exactly where the drawing room was, but once she heard voices, she simply followed the sound.

She came to a large room at the end of a hallway and saw that there were polished dark wooden bookcases lining the walls and several blue velvet sofas scattered around the room. There were also four people staring at her quite intently as she entered the room.

An older handsome man, who she assumed must be Ward Redfield—her father, stood by one of the sofas. He'd been mid-conversation with a much older woman whom she guessed was his mother. Two younger women, roughly about Eliza's age, or perhaps a few years younger, sat on the sofa near them. After an initially awkward moment of silence, the man took a step towards Eliza, smiled and held out his hand.

"You must be our Eliza?" His eyes were kind, and dark blue-gray. The same shade as her own. She stared at him in wonder, noticing that they also shared a similar straight nose and chestnut brown hair with a distinctive widow's peak. Her mother did not share that hairline, though the color was the same and their lips were similarly shaped— people often remarked that their smiles were almost identical. Eliza was surprised to discover that she looked more like her father than her mother. It was something she hadn't considered at all.

The older woman stood and walked over to them. She glanced at her son and then introduced herself. "Hello, dear. I am your grandmother. You really do favor your father. It's quite remarkable."

Eliza nodded. "Thank you. It's lovely to meet you." She glanced at her father and quickly added, "Both of you. As you can imagine, this was all quite unexpected."

Her grandmother cocked her head and regarded Eliza intently. "Your mother never mentioned your father? All these years?"

"Not in any specific way, no. She always just said he was a lovely man. A gentleman, but that he wasn't able to be in our lives. She never explained more than that. She tried to, before she passed, but she waited too long and was too weak. Lady Ashton said that she managed to send a letter before she passed."

Her father nodded. "She did indeed. Your mother was a special woman. If I'd known sooner…"

"What's done is done," his mother said quickly. "I am very sorry for the loss of your mother."

"Yes, very sorry. She was much too young," her father added.

"Come, meet your sisters," her grandmother said as she took a step toward the two women on the sofa who were watching them with interest. Both women had blonde hair that wasn't quite curly but also wasn't quite straight. It was wavy and wiry and both of their carefully styled updos had loose strands that gave Eliza the impression that one wrong move and the rest of their hair would break free and go every which way. She also noticed that while both women were attractive, with blue eyes and fair skin, neither of them looked as much like their father as Eliza did.

Their dresses were beautiful and made of the finest fabrics. Alice was wearing a shimmering bronze confection and Rose was in an elegant burgundy velvet sheath dress with a creamy strand of pearls.

"Half-sister," Alice corrected their grandmother.

"And how do we know she's not making this up?" The other asked.

Both women glared at her with icy distaste. Her grandmother shook her head.

"She looks more like her father than either of you do. How can there be any doubt? Now, please welcome your sister more civilly."

Rose sighed. "Fine." She forced a smile. "It's ever so lovely to meet you." The sarcasm was evident.

Eliza was taken aback. "Thank you. It's lovely to meet you both as well." She tried to keep her voice steady. Eliza didn't know what she'd expected, but to be greeted with such rudeness by her sisters was both a shock and a disappointment.

Alice leaned forward, a sly look upon her face. "Is it true you've been working as a ladies' maid?"

"Alice!" her grandmother scolded her.

"Yes, it's true. I was a ladies' maid." Eliza stood a bit taller. "And I was a very good one."

"Of course you were. But things will be different for you now," her father assured her.

Her grandmother looked thoughtful. "There will be an

adjustment period. It will have to be managed quite carefully."

Daniel, the young footman that Eliza had met earlier, stepped into the room. "Dinner is ready to be served."

Her grandmother smiled at Eliza. "Let's all go into dinner and get to know each other a bit more, shall we?"

5

*D*inner lasted for nearly two hours. Courses came out slowly as the footmen waited until her grandmother was completely finished with each course before removing the plates and bringing out the next course. And since her grandmother did most of the talking, it took time for her to finish her food.

Everything was wonderful, though Eliza was grateful that the portions were small because she finished every bite and she wasn't used to eating like this. Her grandmother was a skilled conversationalist and included everyone at the table. Eliza learned quite a bit during dinner.

"By any chance did you run into the Archibalds onboard the ship? The Duke, Duchess and their son, Lord Nick Archibald, usually arrive in the city this time of year," her grandmother asked.

Eliza noticed that Alice looked her way at the mention

of the Archibalds. She'd been distant through dinner thus far.

"Yes, I met all of them. I was actually seated with them at dinner. They mentioned that they'd attended gatherings here and looked forward to seeing you all again."

"Did Nick say that? That he was looking forward to seeing... us?" Alice asked.

Eliza nodded. "He did. He said that most of the same people go to all the same parties, so he was sure he'd see us all soon."

"Yes, he will see *us* soon." The chill was back in the air and Eliza got the distinct sense that if it were up to Alice, that *us* would not include Eliza.

"Perhaps it might be best if I arrange a gathering sooner rather than later? That might be the most advantageous way to introduce Eliza to everyone."

"The Archibalds will be invited, of course?" Alice said.

"Yes, of course. I'll meet with Mrs. Smith tomorrow to discuss the details."

"If you like, I can show you around the city a bit tomorrow?" Her father suggested.

"Where will you go?" Her grandmother seemed surprised.

"Well, everywhere. I thought I'd show her Central Park, of course, and I thought she might like to see Macy's and the other shops, and maybe stop by my office and show her what I do all day. Luncheon after at Delmonico's."

"That's quite an itinerary. You've thought this out. Perhaps the other girls might want to join you?" Her grandmother glanced at her sisters, who both recoiled with horror at the thought.

"I don't think so, thank you. We've seen all those places and I most certainly have no interest in going to father's office. How boring."

"Even if we wanted to, we have plans already. The McCarthy sisters are having a luncheon."

"Ahhh, the McCarthy luncheon. You wouldn't want to miss that," her grandmother agreed. Eliza wasn't sure, but she thought she detected a slight note of sarcasm.

"Is that when you all plan the season's parties?" Her father asked.

"Yes, it's when Mary McCarthy gives her approval on the dates. I suppose you might as well tell her we would like the Saturday three weeks from today."

"So soon?" Rose seemed surprised.

Her grandmother nodded. "The sooner the better, I think. And remember what we all agreed on—Eliza is your cousin. From your Uncle Theodore, rest his soul."

"You had a brother? How long ago did he pass?" Eliza glanced at her father with sympathy.

"It has been almost ten years now. Teddy married an English girl, Lady Annabelle. He loved living in England, but he was always a bit sickly."

"It's quite convenient for us that he decided to live there," her grandmother said.

"Yes. It makes our story quite believable. Still, it's a shame we can't just tell the truth. I'd love to introduce you as my daughter," he said wistfully.

"Your bastard daughter. That would be a fascinating introduction to Manhattan high society," Alice said.

"I actually quite like it—if it weren't for the fact that it would be disastrous for all of us. Pity," Rose added.

"Girls," her grandmother warned them.

"Like it or not, Eliza is your sister. I expect you both to treat her as such," her father said.

Her sisters didn't respond to that and mostly stayed silent for the rest of the meal. It was clear that they were not happy to see her and were not going to make things easy for Eliza as she tried to adjust to her new role.

When dinner was finally over, Eliza agreed to meet her father for breakfast the next morning. In spite of her sisters, she was looking forward to the next day and seeing the city with her father.

Later, while Miriam was helping her undress, she asked how the evening had gone.

"Was it what you expected, miss?"

"In some ways, yes. In others, no. I don't think my cousins were as excited to see me as I was to see them," she admitted.

"Has it been a long while since you've seen them?"

"Yes. I was so young when I last saw them that it's almost like meeting two strangers."

"Well, you are so beautiful, miss. Perhaps they are a bit... intimidated?"

Eliza almost laughed at the thought. No one had ever called her beautiful before. It made her wonder though if there was a bit of jealousy that was driving their actions.

There had never been a reason for anyone to be jealous of her before. She sighed. It was all a bit overwhelming, and she was exhausted. She'd had two small glasses of wine with dinner and that, combined with the long journey, had finally caught up with her. Miriam wished her a good night and slipped out the door. Eliza crawled into bed and soon after she laid her head on the soft pillow and pulled the blankets over her, she almost immediately drifted off to sleep.

6

*E*liza rose the next day when the sun streamed through the open window. Miriam arrived a short time later and helped her choose a dress for her day exploring the city. She met her father downstairs. He was already in the dining room, reading a newspaper and drinking coffee. He looked up when he saw her.

"Wonderful, you're an early riser, too. Your sisters won't be up for several hours yet."

Daniel stood at attention and once Eliza was seated, he came over and asked if she would like him to pour her some coffee.

"Yes, please. Thank you, Daniel."

"I'm having eggs and toast. You could have the same or something else. They'll make anything you like," her father said.

She smiled. "Eggs and toast are fine."

An hour later, they went outside and Harry pulled the

carriage around to take them downtown. He drove them first to Central Park and her father explained the history of it. Eliza was suitably impressed.

"There's so much green in the middle of this busy city."

"It's really something, isn't it?" Her father stood a bit taller, his pride evident as he watched her taking in Central Park.

"I've never seen anything like it."

They drove by Macy's next and Harry waited outside while they went in and strolled around. Eliza was fascinated. The store was massive and had everything anyone could possibly imagine. So, this was what Harry was talking about.

"You should see it at Christmas. The whole place is decorated. Every year is bigger than the year before."

After they left Macy's, they drove all around the city, stopping now and then so her father could explain the history of what they were seeing. They reached his office building, and he led her inside and introduced her as his niece to several of the men in the office. They were all in suits and sitting behind large desks. Each man had his own office, and they all had a view of the Hudson River.

"What is your business?" Eliza asked.

Her father's eyes lit up. "It's several things, actually. Real estate development is what they all have in common. We buy and sell and build and rent. My father started this business and initially he focused on trading commodities, textiles mostly. And then he expanded into real estate. When he passed and I took it over, we sold the commodities side of the business to focus on the real estate development."

"And you enjoy the work?" It was clear that her father loved it.

"I really do. I love the challenge of building and growing a business. It has had its ups and downs. It hasn't all been smooth sailing, but we're on a good run now. We've doubled our revenues every year for the past five years." He glanced at her outfit and smiled. "That buys a lot of dresses."

Eliza laughed. "That must be wonderful, to love your work." She couldn't imagine what it must be like.

"My father used to say, 'Do what you love and you'll never have to work a day in your life.' I never understood what he meant when I was younger. I do now."

Eliza thought about being a ladies' maid and if anyone really loved that work. She supposed that some must—like Mrs. Smith, who'd spent thirty years with the same family.

"I'd like to learn more about what you do. Maybe there's something I can do to help?" Eliza was used to being on call for most of the day and night, and now with no set duties to fill her day, she worried about how she was going to pass the time.

Her father looked surprised. "You don't have to work. Women generally don't, unless they have no choice."

"Oh, I know. I just thought it might be interesting. To be honest, I'm not sure what I'm supposed to be doing all day," she admitted.

He laughed. "Of course. I forgot for a moment that you

are used to filling your days with work. I don't suppose there's any harm in coming into the office with me a few mornings a week. I could have you help me with some correspondence, perhaps."

"I'd love that!"

"Excellent. Now, what do you say about luncheon? I'm ready if you are?"

Eliza realized that it was already half past noon. "I'm ready."

They went to Delmonico's, and the food was wonderful. Aside from the ship, it was Eliza's first time actually dining in a restaurant. She took in her surroundings—the polished dark wood and crisp white linens on the tables and the waiters, all male, in their black and white uniforms. At her father's urging, they both ordered the steak special and while they ate, her father opened up about how he'd met her mother.

"She was my first love, your mother. We met when my family and I spent a month with the Ashtons. I think I fell in love with your mother the first day I met her. She was beautiful, of course, but there was just something about her. I loved being in her company and I think she felt the same way. I wanted to marry her." He paused for a moment and she saw the sadness in his eyes. "I foolishly imagined it was possible, and I told my parents I'd fallen in love. I expected they might be disappointed but would ultimately agree, but my father strictly forbade it. Things were different then. More so than they are now, though even now I don't think he would have said yes. It just wasn't done."

"Because my mother wasn't a lady?"

He nodded. "Because she was a servant. My father insisted that the classes just didn't mix. I thought it was rubbish then, and I still do. But, I understand it. Society has rules that must be obeyed if one wants to remain in that society. And my parents cared very much about appearances."

"And you don't?"

"Not as much as they did. I'd like to think if I'd known about your mother's situation, about you, that might have changed things. But in all likelihood, it wouldn't have. That will always be one of my greatest disappointments. I missed having you and your mother in my life."

Eliza wasn't sure what to say to that. So, she just nodded and stayed silent. Her father looked deep in thought for a long moment, remembering… finally he took a deep breath and she saw warmth and hope in his eyes.

"But, you're here now. So, let's make the most of the time that we do have. Hopefully a great long time."

Eliza smiled. "I'd like that." So far, she liked just about everything about her father. Her sisters, on the other hand…

Her father seemed to read her mind. "Don't worry about your sisters. They'll come around, eventually. It was quite a shock to them, too."

Eliza hoped he was right, but she had her doubts.

After lunch, they headed back to the house.

"I'm going to drop you here, then continue on back to the office. I have several meetings this afternoon."

He stopped walking for a moment and his expression was thoughtful. "If you're serious about wanting to learn more about the business, you could come in with me tomorrow morning. I have a stack of correspondence that needs to be addressed."

"I'd really love that. Thank you for lunch and for the grand tour. I'm excited to be here."

Her father smiled. "You're very welcome. I'll see you later tonight, at dinner."

When Eliza stepped inside, the house was oddly quiet. She remembered that the girls were out at a luncheon and wondered if her grandmother was out too.

"They're all out," Mrs. Smith said. She'd walked into the main foyer a moment after Eliza arrived and saw the question in her eyes as she glanced around the eerily silent house.

"Your grandmother went to her best friend Thelma's house for afternoon tea. She told me to invite you to make yourself at home, to feel free to explore the house. She stressed that you might want to visit the library, which is on the second floor. It has quite the collection."

"Thank you. I might just do that."

"If you need anything, don't forget to ring downstairs and someone can assist."

Eliza nodded. "How many are on staff here?" She was curious, as it felt so quiet.

"There are about a dozen of us, in a variety of roles.

There's a head chef and scullery maid in the kitchen. Groundskeepers, several footmen, ladies' maids, a butler for your father and, of course, Harry, the driver."

"I was just curious. That's a larger staff than the house I just came from."

Mrs. Smith smiled. "You'll find out soon enough, Eliza. Everything is bigger in America."

7

"*W*hat is she like?" Edna, the kitchen assistant, asked.

Everyone around the table, all twelve servants, looked Miriam's way, eager to hear about the new resident. They'd just sat down to eat supper, as usual, at six sharp.

"She's actually quite lovely. So far." Miriam was a bit in disbelief, half-expecting the other shoe to drop anytime and the ugly side of Miss Eliza to show itself. Surely it must be there? She'd certainly seen it from the other two. They all had. Rose and Alice were pleasant enough—until something displeased them.

"I heard from Harry that she's going to work with Mr. Redfield tomorrow. Harry drove them all around the city today," Lydia, Alice's maid, said.

Miriam smiled. "Mr. Redfield gave her the grand tour. He bought her a beautiful new parasol at Macy's," Miriam said.

The unexpected sound of footsteps coming down the hall drew their attention to the doorway.

"Miss Eliza! What can we do for you?" Canning and the other footmen stood as Eliza tentatively stepped into the room, and she immediately felt regretful.

"I'm ever so sorry to bother you. I didn't realize you were all eating. I thought I could help myself to a cup of tea. But it's not important. Please don't let me disturb you." She turned to leave, and Miriam jumped up.

"Miss Eliza, it's no problem at all. I'll bring your tea right up to your room."

Eliza's face reddened, and Miriam thought it was curious that she was so flustered.

"Thank you. I'm so sorry to trouble you all. It won't happen again." She almost scurried out of the room as the others around the table exchanged glances.

"Miriam, you'll take care of her tea?" Canning asked as they sat back down to eat.

Miriam nodded. "Yes, of course." She took her last bite of stew, then went across the room to boil water for the tea. She could still overhear the others as she prepared a tray for Eliza.

"What was she thinking coming down here?" Lydia asked.

"She was more than apologetic," Mrs. Smith said. "She just needs to learn how things are done here."

"She's a real beauty," Louis said. He was the youngest footman, at only eighteen, and was easily impressed. But Miriam noticed the other men nodding in agreement.

"That's enough," Canning said. "It's not for us to comment on Miss Eliza's appearance."

"Odd that she's going into work with Mr. Redfield. The other two never did that," Lydia said.

"I don't think it's odd," Mrs. Smith said sharply. "I suspect she just wants to spend time with her uncle. It's been a long time since they've seen each other."

"But what could she possibly do there?" Louis asked.

"Women like her don't work," Joe chimed in. "What could she know of Mr. Redfield's business?"

"I believe she offered to help him with his correspondence. Which is a perfectly suitable thing for a young lady to assist with," Mrs. Smith said.

That ended the conversation and Canning changed the subject.

"Mrs. Smith, I understand we'll be hosting a rather large party soon to introduce Miss Eliza. Has a date been set?"

"Mrs. Redfield will let us know tomorrow. It looks like it will be in about three or four weeks."

Canning frowned. "Three weeks? That doesn't give us a lot of time to prepare."

"We'll manage," Mrs. Smith said as Miriam put the kettle of hot water on the tray with a cup and saucer, several tea bags, sugar, and a small pitcher of milk. She lifted it carefully and headed upstairs.

The door was ajar when Miriam reached Eliza's room. She peeked in before entering and saw Eliza sitting at her small table, with her nose in a book. Eliza looked up and immediately apologized again when she saw Miriam.

"Thank you. I'm so sorry. I should have known better. I feel terrible for interrupting your dinner."

"It wasn't an interruption at all. I'd just finished." Miriam smiled and set the tray in front of Eliza.

"Next time I'll ring the bell—but not during your supper hour, now that I know when that is. I just thought I could sneak in and grab a cup of tea without bothering anyone."

Miriam thought that was a curious thing to say. "It's not a bother, Miss Eliza. It's our job."

Eliza nodded. "Yes, of course. Thank you."

"They're having a party for you soon. Mrs. Smith and Canning were talking about it at dinner. It sounds like it will be a grand affair—in your honor."

Eliza didn't look very excited about the party, much to Miriam's surprise.

"Do they have grand parties like that often? What do you think it will be like?"

"Several times a season, usually. They all take turns. It seems quite organized actually. The girls attended a luncheon today, I believe, where they were to discuss and agree on the dates for the gatherings. Though I think this party is an addition to what has already been planned."

"To introduce me." Eliza looked somewhat apprehensive at the thought of it.

Miriam nodded. "It should be marvelous. You'll likely

get a new dress, especially made for the occasion, and you'll meet everyone who's anyone."

"Well, that sounds a bit terrifying," Eliza admitted.

Miriam laughed. "It should be magnificent, a night to remember. The girls always enjoy the parties. They all try to out-do each other. I hear some of the parties can be quite extravagant, decadent even."

Eliza felt a mixture of fear and excitement about this upcoming party. While she was curious to experience such an event, she also worried that she might act in a way that could embarrass her or lead to people questioning her background. She still felt as though she was just playing dress up and that she didn't belong there. She wanted to confide in Miriam, but knew, of course, that was impossible. If the staff ever discovered the truth about Eliza's background... well, she didn't know what would happen. But she knew it would reflect poorly upon her father and his family, and she didn't want that.

"Shall I help you dress for dinner?" Miriam offered.

"Yes, of course. Thank you."

Once Eliza was dressed, she sipped her tea as Miriam arranged her hair. She twisted and pinned it up in a way that Eliza never could have managed herself. As Miriam worked, Eliza asked how long she'd been at the house. She was curious to learn more about her maid, and she guessed that they were about the same age.

"Six years. I started here when I was eighteen. That's when my family moved here from Ireland."

"Do you have any siblings?"

Miriam nodded. "One of each. My brother, Ian, is five years older and my sister, Katie, is a year younger. She's a ladies' maid too, a few houses down. My brother and father work together doing masonry work."

Eliza noticed the small diamond ring on Miriam's wedding finger. It sparkled as it caught the light coming through the window.

"You're married?" She'd been so preoccupied with settling in that she hadn't noticed the ring before.

Miriam smiled. "We just celebrated our one-year anniversary. Colin came over from Ireland, too. He's my brother's best friend. He works here, as well."

That surprised Eliza. "He does? What is his role?"

"He's the second footman."

Eliza nodded. Miriam seemed so young to be married. They were about the same age and Eliza couldn't imagine being married yet. Though it sounded like Miriam had known her husband for many years.

"Do you both live here in the house?" Eliza wondered what it must be like to work together in a house like this. She knew that it was common for romances to develop between staff. She'd seen several couples marry over the years and as soon as they did, they moved into cottages on the grounds.

"We used to, before the wedding. Now we live nearby, in the carriage house behind the main building. It's small, but quite lovely, actually." Miriam's face lit up as she spoke.

"I'm so happy for you," Eliza said. It was clear that

Miriam was madly in love with her new husband. Eliza wondered if she'd ever find that for herself.

"Thank you. Is there anything else I can do for you?"

Eliza turned her head in the mirror and smiled. "I don't know how you do it, Miriam. If I tried this myself, it would be quite the disaster." Her hair had never looked so elegant.

Miriam laughed. "Your hair is easy to work with, nice and straight. Not like…." She quickly stopped what she'd been about to say. Eliza guessed she'd been about to mention her half-sister's flyaway, frizzy hair but caught herself before saying anything negative.

"Well, thanks again, Miriam."

"I'll be back to help you get ready for bed after dinner."

Miriam left and Eliza escaped into her book for the next half hour before it was time to make her way downstairs. She both dreaded and looked forward to it. She was eager to talk to her father and grandmother again, but wasn't looking forward to the rudeness of her new sisters. Maybe they would be on better behavior.

She went to the drawing room first and her grandmother was already there, talking to her father, who immediately stood when Eliza entered the room. The girls hadn't yet arrived. Her grandmother waved her over and Eliza sat next to her on the blue velvet sofa. Her father sat in an adjacent chair.

"Your father was just telling me about your day. How did you like Macy's?"

"Oh, it was marvelous. I've never seen anything like it." London had Harrod's, of course, but Eliza had never been there. She'd only heard of it and imagined it might be similar to Macy's.

"And I trust you enjoyed your luncheon at Delmonico's?" her grandmother asked.

"It was lovely."

Her grandmother nodded. "Your father also tells me that you'll be helping him with some correspondence."

Eliza nodded. "Yes, I'm looking forward to it."

"It must be part-time, though. I know it may seem as though you will have lots of idle time, but once you are introduced, your schedule will quickly fill up with obligations. Luncheons, dinner parties and balls—you'll need to join several charitable organizations—and there will be meetings to attend."

Her father caught Eliza's eye and smiled. "She'll still be able to do all of that. I'll just keep her busy in the morning and she'll have the rest of her day free."

"Hmm. We'll have to make that work, then."

A tall, auburn-haired footman stepped into the room.

"Dinner is to be served."

"Thank you, Colin," her father said.

Eliza took a quick glance back at the footman. So that was Colin. He seemed younger than the age Miriam had mentioned. Maybe it was the freckles across his nose. He had a friendly face and when he smiled, his eyes lit up, reminding her of Miriam.

The girls rushed into the room, stray hairs flying every which way as Eliza's grandmother stood and her father took her arm to walk into the dining room.

"And just in the nick of time," her grandmother said with a look of disapproval.

"I'm sorry, grandmother. We have so much to tell you, though."

"I take it the luncheon was productive?"

"It was wonderful. It's going to be such a busy season," Alice said.

"Good. You can tell me everything over dinner."

Once they were all seated and the first course had been served, Eliza's grandmother looked at Rose and Alice. "Tell me everything. What date has been approved? I need to let Mrs. Smith know immediately."

Alice leaned forward. "Three weeks from this Saturday."

Her grandmother looked pleased. "Good. The sooner the better." She glanced at Eliza. "No one will receive you until you have been properly introduced."

"The Van Bingham ball will be the week before," Alice added.

Her grandmother frowned. "She'll have to miss that. I suppose it can't be helped. They always go first. We were fortunate to get the week after."

They spent the rest of the meal talking about people that they all knew except for Eliza. She tried to pay attention, but all the names were a jumble that was impossible to remember. She'd meet them all soon enough, she supposed.

She was glad that her sisters weren't as rude as they'd been the day before. They simply ignored her as they chattered away with her grandmother. Eliza didn't mind, though. She hoped that in time they might warm up to her. She didn't expect that they'd ever be best friends, but she hoped they'd at least be friendly someday.

"Oh, Eliza," her grandmother said as they were about to leave the room. "I'd like you to come with me tomorrow afternoon. I made us an appointment for a fitting. You'll need a new dress for our party. I'm sure you have many lovely ones with you, but this one needs to be really special."

"You were right about the new dress. We're going tomorrow afternoon," Eliza said as Miriam helped her get ready for bed.

"They'll need to get to work straight away. The party is just a few weeks away?"

"Three weeks," Eliza confirmed.

"You'll be very busy after that."

"I wonder. What if they don't like me? Maybe I won't be invited anywhere," she joked. Though she really did wonder. What if her sisters' friends and their mothers didn't think she was worthy? She knew her sisters wouldn't dare share her truth because it would reflect badly on them, but she also sensed they wouldn't go out of their way to help her fit in. It was a bit nerve-wracking.

"Don't be silly. They will love you. And you'll have a beautiful new dress. It will be fun for you tomorrow."

"Thank you. I probably am being silly, you're right. I'm just a little nervous about meeting so many new people at once. But, I'm sure it will be fine. I should be more appreciative."

"Don't worry. Just try to enjoy it all," Miriam advised.

Eliza smiled. "Wise words. Thank you, Miriam. Good night."

After Miriam left, Eliza climbed into bed and snuggled into the soft sheets. Her bed was so comfortable and warm. Compared to her spartan room in London, it was positively luxurious. It still didn't quite seem real how much her life had changed in such a short time.

8

"She's not like them at all," Miriam said as she climbed into her bed later that night. Colin was already beside her and turned off the bedside lamp as she pulled her covers up.

"Not like her cousins, you mean?" He asked.

"Not like any of them. It's the accent partly, of course, and growing up in England. Things are different there. But, it's more than that. She's humble, grateful even. The others have a different way about them."

"Well, if she's nicer to you than those other two, I'm all for it. Mrs. Redfield and Mr. Redfield are fine, but those two girls have their moments."

Miriam laughed. "They can be a bit testy at times. Fortunately, Mrs. Smith assigned me to Eliza, so I don't have to see them much anymore."

"Enough of those girls….come give your husband a kiss."

"If you insist.." She laughed again as Colin pulled her towards him. Work was the last thing on her mind as his lips met hers.

After breakfast the next morning, Eliza and her father set off to his office. Harry drove them and tipped his hat when he saw her.

"Good morning to you both."

"It is a fine morning, indeed," her father said as he took Eliza's hand to help her into the carriage.

"Good morning, Harry. Nice to see you again," Eliza said.

As soon as they were settled, Harry headed to her father's office, which was about a ten-minute ride. They were the first to arrive and her father led her into his massive office with the huge windows that looked out on Madison Avenue. The first thing she noticed was a beautiful grandfather clock made of polished dark cherry wood. It stood almost eight feet tall and was the focal point of the room.

"Why don't you sit here?" There was a smaller desk adjacent to his that was empty other than a stack of unopened mail and a sickly-looking green plant. Eliza settled behind the desk and turned to glance out the window. She could see carriages going by and swirls of smoke from one of the nearby factories.

"That mail all came in last week and I haven't had a chance to even look at it yet. Do you want to start by reading through it and sort in order of when each needs a response? Then we can go over it all. When you finish, I may have you draft some letters as well, if you think that sounds like something you'd like to do?" Her father sounded a bit uncertain as he sat behind his desk and opened his ledger.

"Yes, it's perfectly fine," Eliza assured him. She was curious to learn more about his work and eagerly reached for the first letter. As she opened it, she heard voices and footsteps in the hallway. Her father glanced toward the door.

"The others have arrived. We have a meeting shortly, so I'll be in the conference room."

He left a few minutes later to join his colleagues and Eliza turned her attention to the correspondence. There were quite a few invitations to various events and several invoices for services or products purchased. There was also a stack of checks—rent payments from his tenants. She organized everything, stacking checks in one pile, invitations in another and invoices to be paid.

When she finished, her father was still in a meeting. She could hear the low hum of their voices behind the closed door. While she waited, she turned her attention to the window and watched the carriages go by below. It was a busy street, with lots of people walking or riding along. She wondered about their lives—were they all going to work and what did they do? The city was so lively and busy with an energy that was exciting.

"You're finished already?" She turned at the sound of her father's voice as he walked into the room. He sat at his desk and they spent the next hour going through the many invitations—there were business dinners and luncheons and several charity events.

"They invite me because they are hopeful for a generous donation, which, of course, I give." Her father grinned, and she smiled at his good humor.

She handed him the stack of checks and they went through the invoices. She read out the name of the vendor and the amount due. Her father wrote the checks out and gave them to her to address the envelopes and mail them off.

"Do you normally do this yourself?" Eliza asked. It was time-consuming and her father clearly preferred to do other work, so put off dealing with the correspondence until he had no choice.

"I had a young woman that was helping me, until a few months ago when she had her first child and, of course, she's not available any longer. I thought I could manage, and I could, but truthfully, I'd rather not. So, if you don't find it too tiresome, I am happy for the help. If you'd rather not do it, perhaps you could help me find a replacement?"

"Oh, I'm more than happy to help. I'll get these checks posted immediately."

"Thank you. I do mean it though. If this starts to bore you, please let me know."

Eliza smiled. "I'm not bored."

As she finished addressing the envelopes and stuffing the checks into each one, Eliza listened to the various conversations as different men strolled into the office to talk to her father. He introduced her to them as his niece and they were friendly and welcoming. She listened as they then spoke with her father about the current projects. She found it fascinating. One development project was stalled as they were waiting for zoning approval for the commercial apartment building they hoped to construct. Meanwhile, another project was gathering bids from several contractors and there were pros and cons to each vendor.

When she finished, her father explained one of the projects to her before dictating a letter he wanted written to the head of the zoning board. He made a compelling case for why he should be granted approval to move forward with the project. At least it sounded convincing to Eliza.

Before she knew it, the large grandfather clock drew her attention again when it announced the noon hour with an elegant chime. Her father looked up from the architectural plans he'd been studying.

"It's time for you to go. Harry will be waiting for you outside. I'll see you at home tonight." He smiled. "Thank you for your help today. Have fun with your grandmother this afternoon."

Harry waved when he saw Eliza exit the building. The carriage was parked just in front of the entrance, ahead of two others. Eliza made her way over, and Harry jumped down and opened the door for her.

"Thank you, Harry."

"My pleasure." He climbed back into the driver's seat and they set off. "How was your day?" He asked.

"It was good. I helped my uncle go through some correspondence and write some letters."

"And you enjoyed that?"

"I did. It was very interesting to learn about his business."

"Your uncle must have been pleased. I don't think your cousins share that interest."

Eliza laughed. "No, I don't think that they do. They seemed quite horrified at the idea of it when my uncle mentioned it at dinner."

"You're very lucky, in my opinion," Harry said. His tone was wistful. "I think it is an incredible opportunity to better understand his business. Business in general. I used to love to go to work with my father."

"Did you learn a lot from him?" She knew that his father hadn't been gone long, and the memory was bittersweet.

"I did. I soaked up as much learning as I could. If I'd known then that our time would be cut short, I would have paid even closer attention."

The ride home passed by quickly, and when they pulled into the driveway, Harry stopped to let Eliza off by the front entrance.

"Your grandmother said to tell you to join her in the dining room for luncheon at one. And after that, I'll be seeing you again for the drive to Frederick Taylor for your fitting."

Eliza smiled. It still sounded to her like he was describing someone else's life. "Thank you, Harry. I'll see you soon, then."

9

*E*liza was surprised when she entered the dining room at one and only saw her grandmother there. But then she assumed that her sisters were probably running late again.

"It's just the two of us," her grandmother said as she nodded at the table and Eliza saw that there were only two places set. Her grandmother sat at the head of the table and Eliza sat adjacent to her.

"They're off to luncheon with Evie Eldridge. She's Alice's closest friend and a lovely girl... most of the time."

Daniel and Colin served the food, which was a cup of carrot bisque followed by a curried chicken salad on a bed of mixed greens. While they ate, Eliza's grandmother asked how her morning had gone.

"Did you find it interesting? Or dull as dirt? Your sisters have never shown the slightest inclination to learn about your father's business."

"More interesting than I expected, actually." Eliza told her grandmother what her father had explained about the different projects and the zoning challenge. When she finished, her grandmother looked thoughtful.

"Your father always wanted a son. Someone that could work with him and take over the business one day. Fortunately, he has a good team in place. When he does pass, which shouldn't be for a long time, God-willing, the business should be in good hands and you girls won't have to worry about a thing." She smiled. "But I bet he's thrilled that you've taken an interest. Now he has someone besides me to talk to about it."

After they ate, Harry drove them to the dress shop where Eliza and her grandmother were welcomed as if they were royalty. Frederick Lombard, the designer, took Eliza's measurements and held up various fabric swatches, all the while keeping up a running commentary with her grandmother. The colors were gorgeous and the silk was the finest Eliza had ever seen. They decided to go with a shimmery pale peach that took Eliza's breath away.

Mr. Lombard held up a delicate lace in a French vanilla cream that looked exquisite next to the peach fabric.

"We'll accent the dress with lace inserts on the diagonal, which will look just lovely as she whirls around the dance floor," he breathed.

Eliza's grandmother nodded. "That sounds perfect. The party is just over three weeks from now."

Eliza watched Mr. Lombard's face closely, expecting to

see a flash of panic at the tight deadline, but he didn't seem the slightest bit concerned.

"Very good. We'll get started on this right away and will be in touch end of next week to arrange a fitting."

They said their goodbyes and headed outside, where Harry was still waiting for them. Once they were settled in the carriage, Eliza's grandmother instructed him to take them to Macy's.

"You'll need new shoes, of course. Normally, for a special occasion like this, we'd order from Worth and then just have the dress adjusted here. But there's no time for that." She smiled. "I did, however, make arrangements for a spectacular dress to arrive later in the season for you."

Eliza's jaw dropped. "You ordered a dress for me from Worth?" She knew of the legendary Parisian dressmaker, of course, but never imagined that she'd ever be able to wear one of the dresses.

Her grandmother smiled. "All my granddaughters deserve a Worth dress. Your sisters get a new one every year—since they turned eighteen. It's a Redfield tradition."

Eliza felt as though she'd stepped into another world—this life was so different from what she was used to. It still didn't seem real, that things could change so dramatically. She half-expected to wake up and discover it was all a dream.

When they reached Macy's, her grandmother led the way through the giant store to the shoe department.

"These would look lovely on you." Her grandmother handed her a pair of dove gray carriage shoes that had soft white fur at the top and tied in the back with matching satin ribbons. They were beautiful. A salesman measured her feet and brought a pair for her to try. Eliza slid her right foot in, laced up the back, and sighed. They were heavenly—soft and plush, like slippers.

Her grandmother smiled. "We'll take those. We also need something for dancing." Eliza tried several more pairs of shoes and forty-five minutes later they walked out, each carrying a big bag. Her grandmother had found a pair of new shoes for herself as well.

When they arrived home, they walked in the front door and saw two ladies' maids rushing upstairs. Eliza wondered what was going on, that they were in such a hurry. Her grandmother smiled before explaining.

"Your sisters have an important party tonight. Alice especially wants to impress a certain young man who will be in attendance. I believe you've met him, Nick Archibald —Lord Nick Archibald, that is."

Eliza nodded. "Yes, I met him and his parents on the ship."

"She hasn't seen him yet this year. We met Nick and his parents last year at one of the final parties. Alice was quite taken with him."

Eliza smiled. "He's handsome, and charming."

"He is. Though his family has almost no money to speak of. They need Nick to marry well."

That was a surprise. "They seemed quite well off."

Her grandmother sniffed. "Yes, I'm sure they did. They have quite a respectable background and, of course, the titles. They do have that to offer, if one cares about that sort of thing. Many do."

Eliza realized her face must have shown her confusion as her grandmother continued to explain.

"It's a good tradeoff for some. The young lady gains a title and an elevation in society while his family gains access to her fortune. Young Nick will continue courting heiresses this season until he secures a match. I don't expect it will take long."

"Does Alice want a title?" Eliza wondered aloud.

Her grandmother frowned. "I'm not sure what she wants—if she even knows. It might be just a flirtation. I must confess I'm not keen on the idea of him for a grandson-in-law."

"You don't like Nick?" He seemed pleasant enough, fun even.

"It's not that I don't like him. It just makes me hesitate. I'd prefer a pure love match for you girls—on both sides. As charming as he is, how will Alice know if he loves her or is just after her money?"

When Miriam came to Eliza's room to help her get dressed for dinner, Eliza told her all about the shopping trip and the new shoes. Miriam inspected the new arrivals and approved with enthusiasm.

"They're lovely. Just perfect!

Once Miriam started brushing her hair, Eliza grew quiet. It was so relaxing to have her hair brushed and styled. Eliza wasn't used to the luxury yet. Miriam expertly arranged Eliza's hair as she stared out the window, daydreaming.

She wondered about the party her sisters were going to. And she was both excited and nervous about her grandmother's upcoming party. She knew it was when she would meet everyone and her grandmother seemed so sure that after that evening, she would be invited everywhere, along with her sisters. And she would be expected to call on the other young ladies and their mothers. That seemed a bit nerve-wracking.

"Have they left yet for the evening?" Eliza thought she'd heard her sisters' voices just before Miriam knocked on the door.

"They've just gone," Miriam confirmed.

"I bet they looked lovely." Eliza would have loved to see their dresses, but of course they hadn't stopped by to see her and she didn't feel comfortable intruding on them.

"Don't worry, you'll be heading off to the parties with them soon enough. Once everyone meets you, you'll be invited everywhere!"

"That's what Grandmother says. I'm not sure I believe it," Eliza admitted.

Miriam laughed. "I'm sure you will. Your uncle is very well respected in this town. Everyone knows him. And he's good friends with the Astors. Mrs. Astor's approval is everything, you know." Miriam spoke with certainty, yet Eliza had no idea what she was referring to.

"Who is Mrs. Astor? She sounds important."

Miriam laughed again. "She is the most important

person in New York society. She and her friend, Ward McAllister, have a list with four hundred names on it—all the people she deems worthy of being considered part of New York's high society. If your family isn't on that list, you won't get invited to the most desirable events."

"Really? Why is she in charge?"

"Because people allow her to be. She's very influential and very rich."

"I see. So you have to be rich to be on her list?"

Miriam shook her head. "That's only part of it. She cares just as much about who your family is and how long they have been in New York. Old money vs. New money."

The expression was unfamiliar to Eliza and Miriam laughed at her obvious confusion.

"Old money is when your family goes back for generations. New money is when you're newly rich and not from a well-established family," she explained.

"That sounds frightfully snobbish." Eliza didn't think she cared for the sound of this Mrs. Astor. If she ever discovered the truth about her background, she'd probably ban Eliza from attending any gathering. And perhaps she'd hold it against her father, her grandmother and sisters, too. But, she realized that was all the more reason for her sisters to keep her secret and she relaxed a bit. She still didn't like it, though—and there were so many rules of etiquette to remember. She would have to be careful not to make a wrong step.

10

*E*liza didn't see her sisters until the next evening in the drawing room before dinner. They both looked lovely as usual, but tired. Miriam had explained while Eliza was getting dressed that many of these parties went well into the wee hours and that both girls slept late and didn't come out of their rooms until early afternoon. They were unusually quiet and didn't join the conversation at all as her father and grandmother discussed a new real estate project her father was embarking on. Eliza was fascinated by their discussion and had first heard of the project just that morning while helping her father with his correspondence.

"We can make these apartments affordable so that honest working people and their families can live there." Her father was enthusiastic about the new development.

Alice made a face. "Why do you want to cater to those people? Wouldn't it be better to make luxury residences?"

"Better for whom?" Grandmother said sharply.

Her father shook his head. "There's no shortage of fine homes for people like us. There is a real shortage of housing for the middle and lower classes. You should see the conditions of some of the buildings. It's a disgrace."

"If you say so." Alice was decidedly uninterested.

Colin stepped into the room a moment later and announced that dinner was ready. They all stood and made their way into the dining room.

Once they were all seated, Colin poured a small glass of rich Cabernet for each of them, while Daniel served the first course, a wild mushroom consommé.

Grandmother took a delicate sip of the consommé then set her spoon down and looked at Eliza's sisters. "So, how was the party? Tell me everything."

Rose's face lit up. "It was really lovely. There was so much dancing. The music was just wonderful. And the food was decadent. Of course, I couldn't eat much at all because of these horrible corsets."

Grandmother chuckled, "That may be a blessing my dear. It's too easy to indulge in rich foods. Alice, what did you think? Were there any interesting young men in attendance?"

A curious expression flitted across Alice's face and she glanced at Eliza briefly before smiling with satisfaction. "Lord Nick Archibald was there. It was good to see him again. We danced a waltz. It was marvelous."

Grandmother nodded. "His mother informed me that

they'll all be coming to our party. I just received her response this morning."

Eliza noticed that Rose and Alice exchanged glances before Alice frowned and ever so slightly shook off Rose's silent request. Rose looked annoyed and stayed silent and deep in thought for a moment. When she opened her mouth to speak, Alice glowered at her, but Rose pressed on, undeterred.

"I chatted with Nick, too." To Eliza's surprise, Rose glanced her way. "He asked after you and said he's looking forward to saying hello when they come to our party."

Eliza smiled. She was glad to hear it. Nick was her first friend in this city and she looked forward to seeing him, too. She chose her words carefully. "Isn't that nice of him? I look forward to seeing his parents as well."

"And what about you, Rose?" Grandmother asked. "Did you talk to any interesting men? Was there anyone new there?"

"No one new. The same people are at all of these parties, it seems. Almost everyone is spoken for and the ones that are not are... not quite right, for me, that is."

Grandmother nodded. "The season has only just begun, my dear. There are bound to be new people at some of these gatherings. Don't give up hope yet."

Eliza's father glanced around the table and smiled fondly at his three daughters. "Your grandmother is right. Remember that you're all Redfields, and any young man would be lucky to have any of you."

Eliza took a sip of her soup and wondered if that was

true. Finding a husband wasn't something she'd given much thought to. First, she needed to get used to her new position in life and believe that it was secure. She worried at times that she would wake up and discover that it had all been a dream—that her new life had somehow been snatched away from her and she was a ladies' maid in London again. She shuddered at the thought.

11

*M*iriam ate breakfast with the rest of the downstairs staff at six each morning. They ate early, before the rest of the house stirred. Mr. Redfield was usually in the dining room by seven. Eliza joined him most mornings now, while the girls and their grandmother rarely made an appearance before nine and Mrs. Redfield often enjoyed her breakfast in bed.

Miriam glanced at Colin and smiled when she saw that he and Harry were deep in conversation about the textile business. It was all Harry ever talked about—his dream to open a textile factory someday and a store bigger than Macy's. His enthusiasm was contagious even though they all knew the reality of it ever happening was in the very distant future, if at all.

Miriam knew Colin often felt restless too in his role as a footman. It was a secure job, and it paid decently, but it wasn't intellectually challenging and her husband was a creative, smart man. Her brother regularly offered Colin a position with him, working as a bricklayer, a mason. It was a good, honest job, but the pay was about the same and the work was physically much more demanding.

They both dreamed of doing something else, something better. But neither knew what that might be. And truth be told, Miriam didn't mind her work, and she loved the small home that she and Colin shared. Free housing was a benefit that they simply couldn't afford to lose.

"A dozen more acceptances arrived today," Mrs. Smith announced.

Canning looked up from his page of notes. He'd finished his breakfast before any of them arrived and was quietly drinking a second cup of coffee and going through a list with Mrs. Shelby, the cook, for the food they'd be ordering for the party. She shook her head occasionally, and he made adjustments to the amounts of various items.

Canning frowned at the news. "I don't think we've had a single decline. So far, everyone is coming. And she's invited the entire city, it seems."

Mrs. Smith chuckled. "The ballroom is limited to four hundred, as you well know."

"Yes, but this will be the first time we've filled it to capacity." Canning glanced around the table. "This will be quite an undertaking. We'll all need to help make this event a success."

They all nodded. Everyone knew how important these parties were, especially this one. Miriam had heard from some of her friends, who were ladies' maids in other grand houses, that there was quite a bit of curiosity about the new arrival to the Redfield home. Miriam also knew that, while the men were eager to meet a new pretty face, the women were somewhat less enthused and already viewed Eliza as competition.

Because it was whispered that an enthusiastic Nick Archibald had spread the word that Eliza was both beautiful and charming, and as a member of one of the richest families in New York society, she would be considered quite a catch. Miriam was sure that Eliza had no idea about that though, and she suspected she might be quite intimidated, horrified even at the thought of it.

Miriam finished both slices of her toast before taking a bite of the creamy scrambled eggs, made the just way she liked them, with a little cheese and a pinch of chives. For some reason, this morning, her stomach wasn't interested. But she knew she needed to eat, so she forced a few bites down and promptly regretted it. The smell of the eggs was overpowering and after taking a few bites, she had to excuse herself from the table.

Miriam made it to the restroom just in time and vomited until she was dry heaving. She normally had a strong stomach, but it had been sensitive this past week. Miriam wondered if she had some kind of flu as she'd been fighting waves of exhaustion, too. But after running a cool washcloth over her face, she felt better. Hopefully, whatever this was would pass soon. Miriam really wanted to crawl back into bed, but she had work to do.

Four days later, Miriam was still feeling unwell as she

forced a smile and went to Eliza's room to help her dress for dinner. She didn't feel sick exactly. She was just having a hard time keeping anything down. And she was so tired, utterly exhausted. Eliza frowned with concern when she saw her.

"Are you sick, Miriam? You look so pale."

Miriam shook her head. "I may be fighting something. I'm just not hungry and am more tired than usual." She smiled. "I'm sure I'll be myself in a day or two."

"Would you like one of these cookies? We stopped by a bakery after the fitting today and these truly might be the best cookies I've ever had. They're so fragrant—raspberry rose. Try one." Eliza opened the box and the intense scent of raspberry assaulted Miriam's senses. She recoiled and took a step backwards.

"Thank you, but I don't think my stomach is quite up to it."

Eliza regarded her thoughtfully. "In our London house, there was a housekeeper that had a sudden aversion to quite a few foods and she especially had a hard time with strong smells." She looked like she was about to say something more, but hesitated.

"What was wrong with her?" Miriam asked.

"She was with child, her first."

"Oh." That hadn't crossed Miriam's mind at all. Her mother died years ago. There was no one to tell her what to expect.

Eliza smiled. "Do you think that might be it?"

Miriam felt suddenly light-headed from lack of food

and shock at what Eliza had said. She sat for a moment and nodded. "I think it's possible."

Eliza poured a glass of water and handed it to her. "Drink this. You look about ready to pass out."

Miriam took the glass and sipped the water. "Thank you. We've wanted this, Colin and I, but it hadn't happened yet and I'd lost hope a bit."

"Well, this is exciting news, then. Congratulations!"

Miriam went to stand up, but Eliza motioned for her to stay seated. "I think I can manage. Rest and get your strength back."

Miriam nodded gratefully. "Thank you. Once you're dressed, I'll fix your hair. I'm already feeling a bit better." Now that she knew what was wrong, excitement about the baby gave her strength. "How is your dress coming along?" She was sure it would be beautiful. Mrs. Redfield had exquisite taste.

Eliza's face lit up. "Oh, it's the most gorgeous dress I've ever had. It's almost done. They only had to make a few adjustments today and it will be finished early next week. I'm nervous about this party," she admitted. "But I can't wait to wear that dress."

"I'm sure it will look lovely on you. I can't wait to see it." Miriam stood and Eliza looked concerned.

"Are you sure you feel well enough? I'm sure I can do something with my hair. You should sit and rest."

"I'm fine. The feeling has passed." Miriam picked up a brush and got to work. Ten minutes later, Eliza's hair was artfully arranged in a flattering updo.

Eliza admired her hair in the mirror and smiled at Miriam. "Thank you. I don't know how you do it. But if I need to, I can manage. So, if you're ever not feeling well, you must tell me. And you'll tell Mrs. Smith so she can watch out for you, too?"

"I will. I'll let her know as soon as I've told Colin the good news. I'll keep quiet with everyone else though, as it's early on—just in case something goes wrong."

"I won't say a word then until you tell me to. But, I'm so happy for you, Miriam."

12

"Are you excited about the big party this evening?" Harry asked. It was just after one on Friday afternoon and he was driving Eliza home from the office. She'd been working with her father all morning, drafting letters and taking notes during one of his meetings that lasted several hours. Eliza had organized the meeting and arranged for a luncheon to be brought in. There were six men and Eliza and they ate in the conference room, while her father led the meeting and ironed out plans for his new apartment building. The others were resistant at first, but her father managed to persuade them to make most of the housing affordable.

"I think I'm equally excited and terrified," Eliza said and laughed. "I really don't know what to expect."

Harry chuckled. "I expect you'll be the belle of the ball. You're the new girl and all the fellows will want to meet you and claim a dance."

Eliza smiled. "I don't know about that." She hoped it was at least partly true, though. She had visions of herself as a wallflower, watching from the sidelines as all the others waltzed by. That's how it had always been before. She and the other ladies' maids would steal a peek from far off during parties. She'd always dreamed of being one of the women in their beautiful dresses, but she never actually imagined it would happen.

Now that it was about to, she didn't quite know how to feel about it. Eliza just hoped that she wouldn't mess it up too badly. She worried that she might say the wrong thing, somehow give away her true background and ruin everything. And she would hate to bring any kind of embarrassment upon her new family. Eliza took a deep breath. She could do this. She just had to be aware and careful of what she said at all times.

"How are your plans coming along for your business?" Eliza asked Harry.

He grinned. "I'm getting closer. Saving every penny and I've lined up two possible investors. Once I have the financial backing, we'll get the textile factory going and once that's a success, the next step is the department store. It will happen. You just wait and see." His enthusiasm and confidence were contagious.

"I have no doubt that it will," she agreed.

They fell into a comfortable silence for the short remainder of the ride. When Harry pulled up to the entrance and jumped out to open the door for Eliza, he smiled. "Don't be nervous about tonight. They're coming to meet you. Try to enjoy it."

She nodded. "I will. Thank you, Harry." She noticed he had two deep dimples when he smiled, and it gave him a mischievous look. But Harry was still so handsome and kind. She'd grown to enjoy their chats as he drove her to and from her father's office each day. Other than Miriam, Harry was her only other friend. She wished he was going to be at the party. It would be nice to have a friend there. But of course, Harry wouldn't be anywhere near the party.

And Eliza wouldn't know a soul there other than her family and Nick and his family, of course. But she didn't know them well. She knew her grandmother would want her to mingle and her father would be busy entertaining his associates. That left her sisters, and they hadn't shown any interest in spending time with her yet, so it was unlikely that would change this evening. Eliza sighed. She'd put on her stunningly gorgeous new dress, have Miriam fix her hair, and then she'd go downstairs and make the best of it. Maybe, if she was lucky, she might even have fun.

Eliza gasped as she saw her reflection in the mirror. Miriam had helped her into the new dress and worked her magic with an elaborate updo. The overall effect was otherworldly. Eliza twirled and admired her reflection from different angles.

"You look beautiful," Miriam said.

Eliza grinned. "Thank you. It's the dress and your hairstyle. I don't quite feel myself."

Miriam laughed. "I expect you are going to have a lovely evening. I look forward to hearing all about it."

Eliza glanced out the window and saw a line of carriages waiting their turn to pull up to the front door. The guests were arriving. "I suppose I should head downstairs now?"

"Yes, your grandmother will be in the ballroom. The guests will be presented to the family as they arrive."

Eliza made her way down to the ballroom. It was an impressive room, with soaring high ceilings covered in sculpted gold. The dark wood moldings were so polished that they seemed to shimmer in the light of two magnificent chandeliers. The walls were painted in soft pastel shades of light gold and pale blue and the window drapes were a deep midnight blue velvet. The overall feeling was one of opulence. The artwork displayed on the walls was impressive as well, and Eliza stopped to admire several paintings on her way to her grandmother.

Her grandmother was deep in conversation with a woman that Eliza didn't know. Eliza immediately sensed that the woman was someone important though, as her grandmother seemed to be standing a little taller and both of her sisters were listening intently. She was wearing an exquisite silvery gray dress and Eliza had never seen a woman wear so many diamonds. They were dripping off her—enormous earrings, tennis bracelet and an incredible necklace.

"Eliza, there you are. I'd like to introduce you to one of my dear friends, Mrs. Caroline Astor."

Eliza extended her hand and smiled. "It's a pleasure to meet you."

Mrs. Astor smiled tightly and shook her hand. "You as well. Your grandmother tells me you've recently arrived from London?"

Eliza suddenly felt nervous. "Yes, from just outside London."

"And you're just visiting then? Or is this a longer stay?" Mrs. Astor held her gaze and Eliza felt like she was being sized up and perhaps found wanting. She took a deep breath.

"I may stay a while. It has been many years since I've been here, and I'm looking forward to exploring the city." The lie came out smoothly and Eliza felt a bit guilty, but the alternative was impossible, so a white lie was a necessity.

Mrs. Astor stayed quiet for a long moment before she finally nodded and seemed satisfied with Eliza's answer. She spoke to Eliza's grandmother again briefly before excusing herself to say hello to her good friend, Ward McAllister.

"Those two are as thick as thieves," her grandmother said. "Stay here by my side and I'll introduce you to everyone."

Eliza met so many people in the next hour as guests continued to arrive. Like Mrs. Astor, Ward McAllister asked Eliza some politely probing questions. But Eliza's answers seemed to satisfy him, and he ended their exchange with a broad grin.

"Well, it's simply delightful to have another pretty face at these gatherings. One does get tired of seeing the same people over and over. Though I suppose that's by design, so one really shouldn't complain." He laughed as if he'd said something wildly witty and both Eliza and her grandmother chuckled politely. As soon as he'd moved out of earshot, her grandmother leaned over and whispered, "I can't stand that man. Such a pompous... well, he's not my favorite. But you did well. It is better to be on his good side. He's quite influential with Mrs. Astor."

"He is?"

Grandmother nodded. "Yes. You don't have to like them, but if you want to be included and receive invitations to all the parties this season, you must have their stamp of approval. Silly, but very real. He seemed pleased though and Caroline seemed taken with you as well, so you should be fine."

Eliza tried to remember the names of everyone she was introduced to, but after a while, it was impossible to keep up. Her cheeks hurt from smiling so much. But when she saw her first familiar face, she smiled again as Nick Archibald and his parents approached her grandmother.

"It's so good to see all," her grandmother said.

"You as well." Nick's mother smiled at Eliza. "I'm sure Eliza mentioned that we had the pleasure of meeting on the ship. It's lovely to see you again, Eliza."

"Yes, it's most lovely," Nick added. His eyes twinkled as he spoke, and he looked happy to see her as well.

"It is so nice to see you both again." Eliza glanced at Nick's mother first and then at Nick.

"You must update me. How are you settling in? You are breathtaking in that dress." Nick held her gaze for a long moment, though neither his mother nor Eliza's grandmother noticed as they were deep in conversation.

Eliza felt her cheeks flush. She wasn't used to receiving compliments from handsome young men. And Nick looked even better than she'd remembered. He and his mother were both dressed impeccably in the finest fashions. Nick's shirt and tie were a crisp white and his tails a rich midnight blue, which accented his eyes. Eliza tried to gather her thoughts.

"I'm settling in well. I've actually been helping my... uncle at his office in the morning." Eliza caught herself just in time. She almost said her 'father', but thankfully Nick didn't seem to notice the hesitation.

He raised an eyebrow. "So, you're a working girl, then? That's ambitious of you. You don't find it dreadfully boring?" He shuddered and Eliza laughed.

"I find it all quite interesting, actually. And it's something to do. I don't like to sit around."

"I would hate it," Nick admitted. "Numbers and I don't get along. Well, business of any sort really just doesn't interest me. I am personally a big fan of doing nothing. It's quite relaxing." He grinned.

Eliza laughed again. She couldn't imagine he was serious.

"Of course I am kidding. A bit. One does keep very busy

though with all the social obligations. It sometimes feels like a job."

This time Eliza raised her eyebrow at him and he laughed.

"Just wait. After tonight, you might find yourself too busy to help your uncle."

Eliza shook her head at the ridiculous suggestion. "I'm sure I will still have plenty of time to help. I don't want to give that up."

"You really have no idea, do you? After tonight, everything will change for you. And I look forward to seeing quite a bit more of you. You'll be at all the gatherings going forward, I'm sure. And then, of course, there's Newport in the summer."

"Newport?" Eliza hadn't been there, but of course had heard about the Rhode Island seaside town.

"Anyone who is anyone summers there. They call them cottages, but of course they're really waterfront mansions as big or bigger than their Manhattan homes. Have you been to the Redfield home in Newport?"

Eliza shook her head. It was the first she'd heard of it.

"It's magnificent. With a huge lawn that leads to the ocean."

"It sounds lovely." The only time Eliza had spent near the ocean was on the ship. She was curious now about the Newport home and hoped they would spend time there over the summer.

"My mother is beckoning. I must see what she wants.

You'll save me a dance? I must insist." Nick grinned, and Eliza noticed his deep dimples.

"Yes, of course."

Eliza felt her sister's gaze before she saw Alice glaring at her from across the room. Rose was by her side looking in a different direction, but Alice was sending daggers Eliza's way. She knew it was because she'd been talking to Nick. Eliza sighed. She wondered if Alice would be any friendlier if not for Nick. Somehow, she doubted it. She watched with amusement as Alice walked purposely toward Nick and his mother and as soon as she reached them, her expression changed and she was all smiles and sweetness.

"Are you having fun?" Eliza turned at the sound of her father's voice. He'd walked up beside her and she hadn't even realized it.

"Yes, of course. It's quite a party."

Her father nodded. "It's what one does. What is expected. Truthfully, I prefer smaller gatherings, more inti-mate dinner parties. This grandness is something I usually try to avoid. But that's impossible when it's in my own house." He chuckled. "So, I go along with the obligatory party once a season."

"Nick says I'm going to be insanely busy with social engagements after this. Do you think that's true?"

Her father laughed. "I have no doubt." A moment later, he frowned. "Unfortunately, though, you might be too busy to help me. We may need to look at hiring a new assistant."

Eliza shook her head. "No, I'll manage. I really enjoy helping you in the office."

Her father looked relieved and happy to hear it. "I'm very grateful for your assistance. But if it does get to be too much for you, you must let me know."

"I will. I promise."

"Now, have you seen any food come out of the kitchen yet? I told your grandmother to make sure there were some passed hot appetizers."

"I haven't seen anything yet."

"Well, I'm off to the kitchen then. If anyone is looking for me, I'll be back in just a minute."

Eliza felt her stomach rumble a bit as her father went off to find food. She too thought the custom of serving dinner after midnight was quite strange as well, but her grandmother explained that it was the way for all balls.

"Be sure to have a snack before the party or you'll regret it later," she'd advised.

And Eliza was already regretting it. She'd been too nervous to eat earlier. And her corset was tight enough as it was. She hadn't wanted to be even more uncomfortable. But now she wished she'd had a bite of something. She sipped her cocktail, a frothy champagne punch and surveyed the room, trying to ignore the pain in her stomach.

"Eliza, dear, you must meet Will Whittier. His parents are dear friends and Will is just a year older than you. I'll let the two of you chat." Her grandmother had appeared suddenly by her side, and just like that, she flitted off and Eliza swallowed nervously.

Nick was handsome, but the man standing before her was the most beautiful man she'd ever seen. He was almost pretty if one could describe a man that way. Will had the longest blackest eyelashes Eliza had ever seen and his eyes were a deep dark gray, a most unusual shade. His hair was a mass of tangled, bouncy curls in a brown so dark it was almost black. His nose was strong and straight and his lips were full and curled into an amused smile. He held out his hand, and she shook it.

"It's a pleasure to meet you. How are you liking New York so far? I must confess, I love your accent. London, right?"

Eliza nodded. "Yes, just outside London, actually. I am loving the city so far. Have you always lived here?"

He nodded. "Always. My grandfather is from England. I've been there several times."

Eliza wondered if, like Nick, Will didn't have any interest in working. She thought she recalled hearing that his father was big in banking.

"Do you work with your father?" She asked.

His face lit up. "I do indeed. I work in finance at my father's bank. You probably think that's boring?"

She laughed. "No, I think it's admirable. You are lucky to be able to work with him—in a family business."

Will looked surprised and glanced around the room, taking in the lavish, gilded ceiling and moldings. "I agree. I don't take any of this for granted. And I enjoy the work."

"I work in my uncle's office too," Eliza admitted. "Not full-time, just helping him with correspondence in the mornings. I enjoy it, too."

"Good for you!" Will seemed pleasantly surprised before adding. "There are more demands on a woman's time. More social obligations. I expect you'll be quite busy with all manner of engagements after tonight."

Eliza nodded. "That's what I hear."

"It's really quite dreadful." Eliza turned to see a stylish woman standing next to her. She didn't recognize her, but Will clearly did as he immediately laughed and pulled her in for a hug.

"Eliza, this is my cousin, Minnie Greene. She's not your typical high society woman."

Minnie raised her eyebrows. "Hardly." She glanced at Eliza and was quiet for a long moment. "It's nice to meet you. I didn't mean to eavesdrop, but I did overhear you say that you work for your uncle and that you're enjoying it. He has quite an impressive business."

Eliza nodded. "He does. I have a lot to learn, but I am finding it very interesting."

"I worked closely with my grandfather, too. He taught me all about investing and the stock market. I'd be bored silly if I did as most women do and just go to social engagements." She looked around the room before adding, "I almost never come to these parties, but my husband insisted."

"If you ladies would excuse me, I see someone I need to go say hello to. Eliza, you'll save me a dance?" Will asked.

"Yes, of course." Eliza watched him stride across the room to where another equally handsome blond man had just arrived.

"That's Tom Harris. Will's best friend. The two of them are inseparable."

"Are the social events really so awful?" Eliza asked. Everyone so far had mentioned how busy she'd be, but Minnie was the first to say she actually disliked attending them.

Minnie sighed. "Not entirely awful. When I was single, I dutifully made the rounds and did everything that was expected of me. I carried my calling cards, and went to teas, and luncheons, balls, the opera, all of it. I do like the opera."

Eliza smiled. "We're going tomorrow night. It will be my first opera since I arrived."

"There's almost always a ball of some sort after the opera. And that makes for a frightfully late night. Unlike many of these women that sleep in, I'm an early riser."

Eliza yawned and immediately apologized. "I'm so sorry. I'm an early riser too. I'm not used to late nights."

"You may need to get used to it. If this is your first season and they're hoping to marry you off, you'll need to attend as many engagements as possible. Some of it is fun, though. I really didn't mind as much when I was single."

"Have you been married long?"

"Two years. My husband, Ted, is here, but he's off smoking a cigar with some of his friends from the club. I'm here because he asked me to come. He's much more social than I am. He says it's just for business, but I know he really enjoys these parties. I'd rather be home and in bed."

Eliza laughed. "Well, it is late. I can't say that I blame you."

Out of the corner of her eye, Eliza saw Colin enter the room, but couldn't hear what he said. Minnie, however, understood what was going on.

"Oh, it looks like they're waving us into dinner. The food, at least, is always very good at these late-night balls."

They headed toward the tables, which all had placards with each guest's name. Minnie found hers first and turned to Eliza before taking her seat. "If we don't see each other tonight to chat further, I wanted to give you some advice, as I don't know when I'm likely to see you again. Make the most of the opportunity to work with your uncle. Don't give that up to go to a silly party."

"I will. Thank you. It was lovely chatting with you."

Minnie's words stayed with her as Eliza found her seat and sat next to her grandmother at the head table.

"Ah, there you are, dear. Are you having fun? Have you met anyone interesting yet?"

"I was just talking with Will and his cousin, Minnie. They were both very interesting."

"Will is a handsome devil. He's one of the biggest catches this season. Everyone thought he'd be taken last year, but apparently no one caught his fancy. It's time for him to find a wife. Minnie is a bit unusual. She's very smart, almost too smart, some say."

Eliza didn't doubt it. She was curious to know more. "Why do they say that?"

"She's very good with money. Most women don't handle such things, but she does. She has an account of her own at Chemical Bank and a small office. I heard she goes there every day and manages her affairs, researches new potential investments. I'm surprised that her husband allows it."

"She does?" Eliza was impressed.

"Apparently so. She almost never comes to these events. I was surprised that she and Ted said yes. She is not your typical high society lady."

Eliza laughed. "Will said the same thing."

"Well, he's right. I'll introduce you to a few other young ladies your age. You need a friend or two that will go to all the same gatherings. It's more fun that way." Eliza agreed and thought it was interesting that her grandmother realized that she wouldn't have that kind of friendship with either of her sisters. Not yet, anyway. Eliza was still optimistic that it might be possible at some point.

13

The courses kept coming, one after the next, each with an accompanying wine and Eliza was reminded of the elaborate nine-course meals she enjoyed aboard the ship, but the food was even better. Mrs. Shelby had outdone herself. There was a truffle-scented consommé to start, delicately fried oysters, a foie gras terrine, a refreshing salad tossed in a light lemon vinaigrette, roast duck with a rich cherry sauce, a raspberry sorbet to cleanse the palate followed by filet mignon and buttered asparagus. The meal finished with a cheese course and a selection of rich desserts, which Eliza only glanced at.

"No creme de chocolate for you? That's your favorite dessert," Grandmother asked as she dipped her spoon into the rich custard. She was correct. Eliza loved it, but she was about to burst.

"I can't, possibly. I reached my limit."

"You can dance it off. The music will be starting shortly."

Eliza welcomed the opportunity to stretch her legs. As Harry had predicted, she had no shortage of dance partners once the music began.

She danced with an assortment of men. Most were near to her age and a few were a bit older. They were all pleasant enough and most asked the same questions. How was she enjoying New York so far? It was hard for her to focus on getting to know these men when she was trying her best not to step on their toes. Dancing was not a strength—mostly because she'd never had the opportunity to dance like this.

Eliza managed well enough and was relieved when the song ended and her next partner was Nick. It was because of him and the dancing they'd done on the ship that she was able to hold her own. As he took her hand and they whirled around the ballroom, she noticed Alice watching them closely as she danced past them.

"Alice is up next, I believe. Are the two of you great friends yet?" Nick asked.

"Not yet. We haven't seen each other in years. There's a lot to catch up on," Eliza said vaguely. It wouldn't do to let him know her sister was less than enthused to make her acquaintance. Rose, at least, was civil. Alice was still frosty at best. And dancing with Nick wasn't likely to help matters. But refusing to dance with him would have been unspeakably rude, and Nick was a friend. Eliza's good mood was dimmed when she caught another glimpse of Alice's scowling face.

"Are you going to the opera tomorrow night by any chance?" Nick asked as the song ended.

"Yes, we are. I'm looking forward to it."

He grinned. "Good. I'm looking forward to seeing you there, then." His enthusiasm was contagious and Eliza was smiling as she walked off the dance floor. Alice twirled by her a moment later in Nick's arms and shot Eliza a triumphant glance. It was all so silly. She and Nick were just good friends.

"I believe it's my turn for a dance?" Eliza turned to see Will Whittier waiting. She stepped into his arms and he expertly whirled her around and had her laughing the whole time. Will wasn't just a pretty face. She quickly learned he was very funny, and they shared the same sense of humor.

"There's McAllister, smile and nod when you pass. We like to humor him into thinking we care about what he thinks. But he's truly insufferable. Such a snob."

"My grandmother hinted at that. She said it's important to stay on his good side, and Mrs. Astor, too."

"Unfortunately, that's true, as they have access to the best parties. But he's just awful. Rumor is just a year ago, he was found guilty of taking bribes from people who wanted an invitation to one of his parties."

"He charged people money?" Eliza was horrified.

Will nodded. "He told Collis Huntington he'd arrange an invitation for him and his wife to the most important

Patriarchs' ball of the year. And he did, but Mr. Huntington told him at the ball that he wasn't going to pay the $9,000 that McAllister demanded. McAllister threatened to embarrass him in front of the people he wanted to impress —But Mr. Huntington still refused."

"What did McAllister do? I can't imagine someone being asked to pay such a huge amount of money to simply go to a party."

"Well, it was much more than a party. They were introduced to Mrs. Astor. That was to be their entrance to high society. Huntington leaked the story to a newsman, and they were both embarrassed. But McAllister made sure they were snubbed by all society parties after that."

"How awful that one person has so much control."

"Yes, he and Mrs. Astor are two people you don't want to upset. If you care about these things."

"Do you care? Do you love going to all these social engagements?"

"It can be a lot during the high season when there are events almost every day. But I don't say yes to everything. For the most part, it's fun. And it's valuable for me to be visible. It's good for the bank."

"Oh, I didn't think of that."

Will grinned. "A surprising amount of business gets done at these balls. The men often gather for a smoke and talk often turns to business. Relationships are made and deals struck."

"Well, that does sound interesting." Eliza envied him a bit. It was only the men that went off to talk business.

Never the women. She knew most women wouldn't even understand why she bothered helping her father when he could easily hire someone else to do it. But the more she went into the office, the more interesting she found it all. If she had to find a husband eventually, she hoped, like Minnie, that it might be someone who wouldn't mind if she kept busy working after they married.

The dancing continued well into the wee hours and it was almost three in the morning when everyone seemed to tire at once and the music stopped and everyone went home. Eliza made her way up to her bedroom and managed to get herself out of her gown. She and Miriam had practiced earlier and Miriam had offered again to come and help, but Eliza refused. She didn't want to keep her up that late—especially in her condition.

It took her a while, but eventually she managed to get everything off and changed into her soft nightgown and crawled into bed. It had been a very fun evening, and she wondered if she might be pleasantly surprised and find that she enjoyed the social life of a young society woman after all.

14

*E*liza surprised herself by sleeping until almost eleven the next morning. She'd never slept that late before. But by the time she'd gone upstairs and undressed, it was nearly four. She'd probably still be sleeping if not for the sun streaming through the windows. She'd forgotten to close the blinds the night before. She stretched lazily and turned at the sound of a gentle knock on the door.

"Come in."

Miriam stepped inside holding a pitcher of water and set it on Eliza's nightstand.

"Good morning. I thought I would check to see if you were awake yet and if you'd like me to bring up a breakfast tray. The girls and your grandmother always take breakfast in bed after a late night like this," Miriam said.

"That actually sounds wonderful. Thank you." Eliza had never had breakfast in bed before, and she was so warm under the covers. She didn't have the energy to get up just yet.

Miriam smiled. "I'll be right back. I had a feeling you might be ready. Mrs. Shelby is already cooking eggs for everyone."

Eliza sat up and poured herself a glass of cold water. She'd only had a few glasses of wine the night before and was glad she'd resisted the temptation to drink more than a few sips of the many wines that were served with dinner. But she was still tired, and the water began to revive her.

Miriam returned a few minutes later with the breakfast tray and set it carefully next to Eliza. There was a carafe of hot coffee, scrambled eggs, bacon, potatoes, toast and jam. It smelled wonderful.

"How was the party? Did you have a good time?" Miriam asked as Eliza poured herself a cup of coffee and breathed in the scent before taking a sip.

"It was fun." She told Miriam all the highlights from the party, including the rumor she'd heard about Ward McAllister.

"I'm not at all surprised. I've heard stories from my friends. One worked as a maid in his household for a short time. But I should leave you to enjoy your breakfast. When you come downstairs, be sure to check with Canning. You've already received some correspondence this morning."

Eliza took her time drinking her coffee and enjoying her breakfast. It had looked like a lot of food when Miriam set the tray down, but she'd managed to eat most of it. She took her time washing and changing and eventually made her way downstairs. It was nearly one and a gorgeous, sunny day. Eliza thought she might take a walk and enjoy the nice weather. As she went to find her coat, Canning stepped out of his office and smiled when he saw her.

"Miss Eliza, you've had a number of invitations arrive this morning." He handed her a thick stack of envelopes. There were at least a dozen of them.

"These are all for me? Already?"

Canning chuckled. "This is just the beginning, my dear. Shall I bring you a cup of hot tea in the drawing room?"

"Yes, thank you." Eliza took her correspondence into the drawing room and sat at a small rolltop desk. She opened her first letter. It was an invitation to a tea the following Wednesday afternoon at four, given by Lillian Rhodes and her mother.

"Your tea." Canning announced as he entered the room and set the cup and saucer and pot of tea on the desk. He'd also included several raspberry shortbread cookies. Not that Eliza needed them, but it was hard to resist if they were sitting in front of her.

Eliza looked up and smiled, "Thank you so much, Canning."

As he walked off, she reached for a cookie. She remembered meeting Lillian the night before. Her grandmother had introduced them.

"Lillian is about your age. I thought the two of you might have some things in common." Her grandmother had immediately wandered off and Eliza and Lillian laughed and chatted for a few moments before Lillian's mother arrived and insisted on introducing Lillian to someone. They hadn't talked long, but Lillian had seemed nice. Eliza looked forward to getting to know her better at her tea.

She opened the rest of the envelopes. There were several more invitations to teas, a few luncheons, and the rest were parties and balls. She noticed that nothing started before two in the afternoon, which was a relief. She wouldn't have to miss work yet. She recognized all the names on the invitations. They were all people she'd met the night before. She thought it a bit funny that she barely knew these people, yet they'd so quickly added her to their guest lists.

And tonight, she'd be attending the opera for the first time. Once again, she marveled at the strange, yet fascinating, turn that her life had taken.

15

*E*liza went out for a long walk. It was a beautiful Saturday afternoon, and they weren't going to the opera until much later, so she had the whole day to explore. She decided to head to the Ladies' Mile shopping district. Macy's was located there, along with another big department store, Bloomingdale's and other shops. She knew that it was considered safe and appropriate for women to shop unaccompanied there and she was eager to take her time browsing. She'd only been to Macy's twice, with her father and grandmother, and while she'd enjoyed the experience, she looked forward to going alone and leisurely exploring the shops. There wasn't anything she particularly wanted, but she'd brought her purse and money just in case she saw something she couldn't resist.

Eliza had never been much of a shopper. Working as a ladies' maid limited one's social life and there wasn't a need for fancy clothing or accessories. And they didn't live near anything remotely similar. Harrod's was in London, far from the Ashtons' home. And since Eliza had never been there, she didn't know what she was missing. Because she didn't spend much money, she'd managed to save almost all of her pay over the years. After chatting with Minnie and learning how passionate she was about investing, Eliza wanted to learn more about it. Maybe she could put her savings in the bank or into bonds or stocks. Maybe she could ask Minnie for some advice.

The Ladies' Mile district was swarming with women when Eliza arrived. She made her way through the crowds to Macy's and stepped inside. She looked around, a bit in awe of the high ceilings and the array of sumptuous clothing. The store was large and sprawling, and she happily lost all track of time as she wandered from department to department. It was truly a magical place. Eliza didn't need a thing, but there were so many beautiful items she was very tempted to purchase. But she decided to visit Bloomingdale's first before making any decisions.

Eliza was almost at the entrance to Bloomingdale's when she heard a familiar voice call her name. It was Harry.

"I'm surprised to see you out and about today." He'd mentioned earlier in the week that he had the afternoon off but would be driving them to the opera that evening.

Eliza laughed. "It was a late night, so I did sleep in. But I wanted to get out and do something. Are you enjoying your day off?"

"I am. I just had a nice visit with my mother and

cousins and now I'm poking around my favorite area. This is where I'll have a store of my own one day."

"Right here in the Ladies' Mile?" Eliza smiled. The hustle and bustle of the busy shopping district definitely suited him.

He nodded. "Right here. Macy's, Bloomingdale's and one day Ford's will be here, too."

"I have no doubt it will," she assured him.

"Where are you off to now?"

"I just explored every inch of Macy's. Now I'm off to do the same to Bloomingdale's. What about you?"

"I was actually heading in there myself. I visit these stores almost every week and I learn something new each time."

"Really? Maybe you can show me around."

"Right this way." Harry held the door open and Eliza stepped inside.

The store was beautiful and had a similar feel to Macy's. Eliza followed Harry around the store as he explained how the stores differed.

"They're not that different, really. They are both trying to reach the same customers and they have a wide variety of merchandise. But, with the clothing... feel this." He held the sleeve of an elegant dress up and Eliza touched the fabric. It was high quality and felt nicer than she expected.

"Bloomingdale's has some higher quality products. More expensive too," he said.

"Which direction do you want to go in your store?" Eliza was curious.

Harry grinned. "I want to have it all. There will be some bargains, but I want to be known for quality too. And because we'll be making much of the clothing ourselves, we can pass that savings along. And I got some good news today." His eyes lit up and Eliza had a feeling she knew what he was going to say.

"You got your funding?" she asked.

"Yes. It's still a few months out, but I've secured two investors and we've found the perfect space for the factory. It will be available in two months. It's really happening." She could hear the excitement in his voice.

"I'm so happy for you, Harry. I'll miss you, though."

"I'll miss you, too." He held her gaze for a long moment and looked as though he was about to say something else, but just sighed instead. A clock on the wall chimed the time and Eliza was surprised by how late it was.

"I should probably head back," she said.

"I'll walk with you."

As they walked home, Harry told her all about his visit with his family. He had two younger sisters that both lived at home, several cousins that lived nearby, and his mother and grandmother.

"I bet your family is excited about your new venture?"

He nodded. "They are. My mother is going to work there. She'll be the head seamstress and will oversee the others. And my sisters will join us too. They're both great at sewing and already work at local factories. They'd rather work for me."

"That's wonderful. It's nice when family can work together."

"You're still enjoying going into the office with Mr. Redfield? I wondered if you might get bored with that now that your invitations are coming in."

Eliza laughed. "I couldn't believe the stack that came already this morning. Teas and luncheons and parties. I will be very busy indeed. But I will still make time to help my uncle most mornings. As long as I don't go to many balls like the one last night. We were all up until three in the morning!"

Harry smiled. "I don't doubt it. I knew you'd be the belle of the ball."

"I don't know about that. But it was fun. It would have been more fun if you'd been there. I really didn't know many people."

Harry chuckled. "I don't think I'll make the guest list for any of these balls, unfortunately. You'll get to know people soon enough."

"I suppose I will. It just seems unfair, the way things are." It didn't feel right that Eliza was part of a world that Harry would likely never be welcomed to.

"It's just the way things are. Nothing we can do about that. I do agree with you, though. It does seem unfair at times."

Eliza sighed. She had so much to be grateful for, but it did seem entirely unfair that the one person she liked the most could never be more than a friend. Harry was the only one that made her heart flutter. And now that he was leaving in two months, she probably wouldn't even see him much anymore. The thought was depressing. She tried to focus on the positive though and they spent the rest of the walk laughing and talking non-stop. Before she knew it, they were home.

"This is where I leave you." Harry glanced at the front door and seemed reluctant to go, too.

"Thanks for keeping me company this afternoon," Eliza said.

"It's always my pleasure. I'll see you all later this evening." Harry waited until Eliza reached the front door before tipping his hat to her and heading toward the back entrance.

Eliza walked through the front door, feeling relaxed and happy after spending the afternoon with Harry. The first person she saw was Alice, who was glaring at a stack of correspondence on a side table. Alice transferred her icy stare Eliza's way while Canning stood by, looking uncomfortable.

"Did you say all of those invitations are for.... her?" Alice snapped at him.

"That's correct. These are for you." He handed her a much smaller pile, maybe three or four envelopes, and added, "You've probably already been invited to the other parties."

Alice lifted her chin. "You're absolutely right! I'm sure that I have." She took the letters and stomped off without saying a word to Eliza.

"I think Miss Alice is still a bit... tired. It was a late

night for all of you." Every time Eliza had seen Alice the night before, she had a full glass of champagne. She suspected Alice was feeling quite… tired indeed.

"Thank you, Canning. I'll take these up to my room."

She went upstairs, sprawled on her bed, and read through the invitations. More teas, a few luncheons, and a note from Nick.

"It was lovely seeing you again last night. I am looking forward to our evening at the opera tonight. I believe our box is next to yours. Most sincerely, Nick Archibald."

Eliza smiled. It would be fun to see Nick again. However, she imagined Alice would be even more enraged if she realized he'd sent Eliza correspondence. Somehow, she didn't think Alice would understand that they were just friends. She would have to walk a tightrope tonight—being friendly with Nick without giving Alice the wrong idea about the nature of their relationship.

16

"You're sure we have to go to this blasted party after the opera? I was looking forward to a relatively early evening," Eliza's father complained.

Eliza immediately heard a soft chuckle from the front of the carriage—from Harry, as he drove the family to the Metropolitan Opera House.

"It's not like we have a choice," her grandmother said. "When Caroline Astor invites you to one of her impromptu midnight suppers, you go. I suppose it is my fault, though, for mentioning that we were all attending this evening's opera."

Her father sighed. "It's fine. I know you don't enjoy these late evening events much more than I do."

"Well, I enjoy them!" Alice interjected. "I'd much rather go to one of Mrs. Astor's suppers than to the opera itself. Does anyone actually enjoy opera?"

Rose nodded in agreement. "All the most important and interesting people will be at this supper."

"Well, I, for one, enjoy the opera. It's Faust tonight. One of my favorites," her father said.

Her grandmother smiled. "I enjoy it as well. What about you, Eliza? Do you enjoy opera?"

All eyes turned her way and Eliza shifted uncomfortably. "I've actually never been to an opera before. I am looking forward to it."

Her father's face lit up. "Oh, my dear, you are in for a treat. And to think, your first opera will be Faust. That is just marvelous." His mood seemed to be improving. Eliza smiled and relaxed a bit. Alice and Rose had already looked away and were whispering to each other.

Harry pulled onto Broadway and a few moments later reached the front entrance to the Opera House, where he stopped and jumped down to help them out of the carriage. When he took hold of Eliza's hand, his eyes met hers, and his smile was big and warm. "Enjoy the opera. Faust is one of my favorites too."

Eliza thanked him and watched as Harry climbed back into the carriage and drove off, his dark curls dancing in the wind.

Eliza's grandmother led the way to their seats. The Redfield family had one of the best private boxes in the Metropolitan Opera House. Eliza was dazzled by the beauty of the theater and the people attending—everyone was wearing their finest clothes. She was glad that she'd let Miriam choose her dress. It was made of a stunning midnight blue shimmery fabric. Eliza had wondered aloud if it might be too much. That made Miriam laugh.

"I don't think it's possible to be overdressed for the opera. There are almost always parties immediately after," she'd said.

And, of course, she was right. Alice and Rose were wearing equally exquisite dresses. Alice's was a pale ice blue that complimented her very blonde hair, while Rose wore a dusty pink dress that looked lovely with her elegant French twist. Both girls had hardly said a word to Eliza, but that was nothing new.

Her grandmother patted the seat next to her own. "Sit here my dear." Eliza settled in next to her while her father and sisters sat in the row immediately behind them.

"Nick!" Alice called out excitedly and Eliza turned to see that Nick and his parents were entering the box to their immediate right, along with an older couple that she didn't recognize.

"That is Joe and Bertha Lenox," her grandmother explained. "They're cousins to the Archibalds. They had another engagement and weren't able to attend our party. The Archibalds stay with them when they're in Manhattan."

Nick waved to all of them and winked when he caught Eliza's eye. They were too far apart to have a real conversation, but she knew there would be an intermission and they might have time for a chat then and possibly after the show as well, if his party went to the Astor supper.

"And to your left is the most eligible young man of the

season." Eliza's grandmother glanced at Will Whittier and his parents as they sat in the box to their left.

"Is he really considered the most eligible? I met him at the party and enjoyed talking with him."

Her grandmother nodded. "Will's father, Raymond Whittier, is believed to be the richest man in Manhattan—though your father is right behind him," she said proudly. "He's also expanded from banking into real estate development, and Will is expected to take over the family business someday. We expected he might take a wife before now, but Will surprised everyone and hasn't proposed yet."

She paused for a moment, then lowered her voice, "Alice set her sights on him last season, but unfortunately he didn't seem interested in her or Rose or anyone else, for that matter. There was a rumor that he took a shine to Clara Anderson, but she ended up engaged to someone else."

Eliza didn't know who Clara Anderson was, so her grandmother's gossip was just mildly interesting. Alice had clearly given up and moved on to Nick, and Eliza hoped her sister would realize that Eliza was no threat—she wasn't interested in Nick as anything other than a friend. She did enjoy talking to him though, as he was one of the few people she knew and considered a friend. Hopefully, once she attended some of the teas and other engagements she was invited to, she would meet more people.

She glanced Will's way. He was intriguing and so stylish. Nick, of course, was dressed well, too, but Will had a certain flair about him. Eliza had a good eye for fashion and fabrics and she could tell that Will's suit was of a very high quality. The cut of his black jacket was perfect and his waistcoat was of an intriguing dove gray embroidered fabric that offered a nice contrast to his crisp white shirt and bowtie. He caught her eye and smiled just as the lights went down and the music began.

And for the next hour or so, probably longer, Eliza was spellbound....by the music and the story and the costumes... all of it. When the act ended and the lights came up, she needed to take a moment to reorient herself.

"What do you think of it so far?" Her father asked.

Eliza turned to face him and was surprised to see that Alice had already left her box and was visiting with Nick and his family.

"It's really lovely. I'm enjoying it even more than I'd imagined."

"Excellent." He looked pleased to hear it.

"Shall we stretch our legs, ladies?" Her grandmother asked. Eliza and Rose stood and followed her out of the box and through the politely chattering crowd until they came to an area where champagne was being poured.

"Join me in a glass?" Their grandmother announced. It wasn't really a question, so Eliza and Rose just nodded. A moment later, they took their champagne and wandered around a bit. Her grandmother saw many friends she needed to say hello to and made sure to introduce Eliza to anyone that she hadn't met already. Eliza remembered some of them, but it was helpful to hear their names again.

"What do you think of all of this so far?" Rose asked.

Their grandmother was deep in conversation with a friend. Rose and Alice had hardly spoken a word to Eliza since she'd arrived, so the question took her by surprise. She wasn't entirely sure what Rose was asking.

"The opera? It's lovely."

"No, not that. Society itself, living here. Is it very different from what you are used to?"

That was a loaded question. Eliza chose her words carefully. "In some ways, yes. In others, not at all. The people are different, of course. Everyone seems quite nice."

Rose nodded thoughtfully. "People always seem nice at first, though, don't they? It takes time to really get to know someone."

Eliza smiled. "Yes, I suppose it does."

Rose was quiet as they walked back to their box and didn't speak again until they walked by the Archibalds' box. Alice was still chatting with Nick, smiling and laughing at something he'd said.

Rose nodded their way and spoke softly, so only Eliza could hear. "Things seem to be going well for Alice. I hope no one gets in her way." Rose held her gaze and Eliza felt a chill. The message was received.

"I'm happy for her. For both of them. Nick seems like a great fellow," she assured her.

Rose looked like she was going to speak again, but the lights flashed, indicating it was time for everyone to return to their seats for the next act. Alice rushed back to her seat just as the music began. Eliza quickly lost herself in the story until, too quickly, it was over. Her grandmother stifled a yawn as the lights came up and they stood to leave.

Harry was out front, waiting for them, and drove them home so that everyone could change into more appropriate attire. Eliza's grandmother had explained that, although a supper sounded like a small gathering, Mrs. Astor's after-opera event was more like a ball with nearly four hundred expected to attend.

Miriam was waiting when Eliza reached her room. She helped her get out of her lovely gown and had selected another, even nicer one for Eliza to wear. This was one of Lady Caroline's most exquisite—a peach confection with shimmery gold embroidery across the bodice. It was flattering on and Eliza felt a bit like a princess as she twirled in front of her mirror. It seemed so strange to be heading out to a supper so late in the evening. But she knew this was just how things were done. And she needed to act as though she was used to the extravagance, that it was all perfectly normal. Even if it was anything but.

17

Mrs. Astor's supper was every bit as grand as the excessive party that her grandmother had given to introduce Eliza to society. Everyone was in their finest gowns and tails. Eliza took it all in, the impeccably glad footman gliding by, elegant music playing softly and the swish of dresses as the ladies entered the room. Mrs. Astor looked resplendent in a gorgeous midnight blue dress with diamonds dripping from her ears and around her neck and wrists. For Mrs. Astor, this was just another evening out. Eliza's grandmother told her on the way over that Mrs. Astor entertained like this regularly, and sometimes on very short notice—if she decided to attend the opera, she would quickly arrange for a supper following.

Eliza glanced around the room. There had to be close to four hundred people in attendance. More of a grand ball than an intimate supper. Once everyone arrived, they all sat down to an elaborate meal with nine or ten courses.

Eliza lost count. The plates of food kept coming and coming. The portions were small, thankfully.

The footmen served many wines as well, but Eliza only took a few sips of each. There was just so much, of everything. The food was exquisite—there were many dishes she'd never tried before. She wasn't actually sure what some of the courses were, but she tried a taste of everything and found it all mostly delicious.

She sat next to her grandmother and across from Rose and Alice. Her father was next to her grandmother and, to Eliza's delight, her new friend Minnie was seated next to her.

"I didn't know you were going to be here," Eliza said.

Minnie smiled. Her husband, Ted, was deep in conversation with the man beside him.

"Ted wanted to come. We bought the tickets ages ago, and he happened to mention it to Mrs. Astor when she came into the bank last week. An invitation to the supper arrived the next day. And you know one can't say no to Mrs. Astor."

Eliza laughed. "I'm so glad you're here."

Minnie looked thoughtful for a moment. "You know. I'm having a few people over for a casual supper next week. Ted is going out of town on business, so I thought I'd invite some of my girlfriends. It really will be casual—nothing like this. Would you like to join us?"

Eliza didn't hesitate. "I'd love to."

After dinner, they moved into the ballroom and the dancing began. Eliza was glad to move around and was happily surprised when Nick found her soon after the music started and whisked her off to the dance floor. She was glad to see him but immediately felt Alice's glowering stare a moment before she stepped onto the dance floor with Will Whittier.

"I didn't get a chance to speak with you at the opera. Did you have fun?" Nick asked.

"I loved it."

"Did you really?" He looked surprised. "I have to confess, it's not my favorite thing. But I do enjoy the after-party." He flashed his familiar mischievous grin and she couldn't help laughing.

"Of course you do." Eliza liked Nick, though not in a romantic way. And Alice was so keen on him. She wondered if he and Alice might be better suited. Eliza's first thought, based on her own interactions with Alice, was that Nick seemed too nice for her. But maybe Alice would be different with him.

When the song ended, Eliza joined her grandmother, who was sipping a cup of tea and sitting at a small table with a good view of the dancing.

"Alice looks happy now, doesn't she?" Her grandmother commented. Eliza followed her gaze. Alice and Nick were spinning around on the dance floor and Eliza hadn't ever seen her look so pretty. Alice was glowing as she smiled and laughed in Nick's arms.

"They look good together," Eliza agreed.

Her grandmother glanced her way and was quiet for a moment before speaking. "There is a short window of time to find a husband. It's expected that most young women will be engaged by their twenty-first birthdays. Alice turned twenty-one two months ago."

Eliza nodded. "I'm older than that," she said quietly.

Her grandmother smiled. "Yes, but you're new and interesting. And you could pass for twenty-one. No one needs to know differently, my dear. Do they?"

"I suppose not. I'm not a very good liar, though."

"Oh, who said anything about lying? Just don't offer the information. No polite person will actually ask you your age. So, you don't have a thing to worry about."

Eliza was beginning to worry a bit, though. "Is the expectation that I will get engaged this season? What if that doesn't happen?"

"I'm sure you'll have your choice of suitors, dear. But, if you don't find someone, I suppose it's not the end of the world. There are women who never marry. They're called spinsters, but there were times when I have to confess, I have envied them."

Eliza looked at her in surprise. Her grandmother chuckled. "I married very young, at nineteen. My Henry has been gone for nearly twenty years and while I still miss him dearly, I've also enjoyed doing what I please. When one has means, it can be a very pleasant lifestyle, indeed."

Eliza looked around the room at the flurry of people dancing and flirting strategically. She felt a bit like a panicky fish out of water. Getting engaged so soon seemed impossible.

"I know it's expected of me, but I'm really not feeling

anxious to marry. I've only just arrived here. I'm enjoying getting to know you and my father and spending time with him at work."

Her grandmother reached over and patted her hand. "Well, I'm sure you'll change your mind about that. But you'd be very welcome to remain with us for as long as you like. We are your family, after all."

Eliza didn't sit for long. She spent the rest of the evening on the dance floor with a variety of partners. All of them were pleasant enough, though they blurred together after a while. Until Will Whittier found her. He was great fun and made her laugh as they whirled around the dance floor. He knew everyone and told her about many of them in an entertaining way that was somewhat gossipy but not mean-spirited.

He pointed out an older woman who looked vaguely familiar. "That's Evelyn Wamsetter. She's my grandmother's best friend and has tried to play matchmaker more times than I can count. But her taste is dreadful."

The conversation turned to the opera and Will asked what she'd thought of it.

"I loved it. It was my first time, and it was such a treat."

He looked pleased to hear it. "Not everyone truly enjoys the opera. I've seen Faust before and it's one of my favorites." He was quiet for a moment and then surprised her with an invitation. "I'll follow this up formally, of course, but would you be interested in attending a small gathering at my home soon? Some of my good friends enjoy the arts as well, and we've started meeting occasionally to discuss what we've read or seen. And we may have a soloist pay us a visit. It should be an interesting evening."

"I'd love to." Eliza thought it sounded like great fun and she'd heard about gatherings like this, salons, where the purpose was to discuss art and philosophy. She thought of Nick and guessed that he wouldn't be on the guest list. Nick would likely find such a discussion even more boring than the opera itself.

When the dance ended, Will promised to be in touch soon and Eliza looked forward to seeing him again. He was one of the most handsome and charming men in the room. She understood now why her grandmother said he was considered the most eligible young man this season.

18

"Would you like a bit more chicken stew? And another roll? I just took a fresh batch out of the oven. I've plenty of both," Mrs. Shelby offered.

Miriam couldn't believe she'd eaten her lunch so quickly. There wasn't a drop left in her bowl. She normally wasn't a big eater, but she was hungry all the time lately, it seemed.

"If you're sure you have enough, I'd love it." Miriam never took seconds. This was a first. The others all knew she was expecting, though, and Mrs. Shelby especially paid close attention to Miriam's diet.

"How are you feeling?" Mrs. Shelby handed Miriam a full to the brim bowl of stew, followed by a piping hot roll.

"I get sleepy in the afternoon and I've never had an appetite like this before, but I feel well, overall." Miriam smeared a generous amount of butter onto the hot roll and took a bite. Food even seemed to taste better. It was the strangest thing.

Mrs. Shelby nodded. "That's as it should be."

Miriam knew she was lucky and that Mrs. Shelby was really asking about the morning sickness, which had made Miriam miserable for several weeks but had almost stopped completely. When Lottie, another of the housemaids, was with her first child, she was terribly sick almost the entire time. Miriam was grateful it didn't seem to be the case for her.

Lottie had to take a leave of absence and missed months of work. Miriam couldn't afford for that to happen. She and Colin needed every penny that they earned. They both knew that money meant security and while they had housing now, Colin eventually wanted to start his own business and they would need money for that and for a home of their own.

Lottie was Mrs. Redfield's maid and because she didn't want to lose Lottie, Mrs. Redfield hired an additional housemaid who had experience with babies. Once the baby came, the new maid, Ida, took over watching the baby while Lottie worked. She would be able to watch Miriam's child too, which was a godsend. Miriam knew that Mrs. Redfield also hoped that someday, there would be great-grandchildren of her own that needed watching.

"Lydia, Bessie, would either of you like more?" Mrs. Shelby offered.

Miriam's fellow ladies' maids, who served Alice and Rose respectively, both declined.

"Miss Alice was in an unusually good mood last night," Lydia commented.

Lydia and Bessie were only a year younger than Miriam, who recently turned twenty-four. She was the only married housemaid—other than Lottie, who was several years older. Miriam often felt so much older than the other two girls, though, especially now that she was expecting.

"I don't think Miss Rose is all that fond of the opera," Bessie said.

Lydia laughed. "Miss Alice is not a fan, but she said she enjoyed dancing with Nick Archibald at Mrs. Astor's party."

"Miss Eliza said she loved the opera. It was her first time. I think she enjoyed the party as well. She said she saw one of her new friends there, Minnie, something or other," Miriam said.

"She's a bit unusual, I hear," Bessie said. "One of my friends is a maid at her house. She said Miss Minnie does her own investing and heads off to the bank every day. As if it's a job."

"That's quite peculiar. I am surprised her husband allows that," Lydia said.

Bessie chuckled. "I think Miss Minnie does as she pleases."

"I don't know about any of that," Miriam said. "I am just glad that Miss Eliza has made a friend. It can be hard when you are new and don't know anyone. Her cousins haven't been all that friendly."

"Well, can you blame them?" Bessie said. "None of us had even heard of Miss Eliza and she's suddenly the new girl. I'm sure all the men are intrigued by her. I don't think Alice and Rose would mind so much if they weren't all competing for the same prospects."

"Miss Alice doesn't need to compete with anyone," Lydia sniffed. "I'm sure she was the most beautiful girl there. Her dress was simply divine."

Miriam admired her loyalty but thought it was a bit misplaced. "They are all beautiful girls, and they are family. I think Eliza was hoping for a warmer welcome."

"Maybe they will warm up to her. Once the season is over and everyone is settled and engaged," Bessie said sensibly.

"I'm sure you're right." Miriam was anything but sure about that, though. She could only hope that Miss Eliza's cousins would eventually warm up to her.

19

After the whirlwind weekend with the opera and Mrs. Astor's party, and then a quiet day to recover on Sunday, Eliza was glad to head into the office with her father Monday morning.

Everyone in the office was pleasant enough toward her, but Eliza couldn't help noticing a somewhat chilly attitude from Richard Owens, her father's right-hand man. Richard's role was to manage all existing development projects and to report back to her father about any issues that might arise. Eliza didn't know what his problem was with her, but he seemed to regard her with some suspicion. He raised his eyes when she walked into the office with her father.

When her father excused himself to go fetch the morning mail, Richard frowned in her direction.

"So, this is going to be a regular occurrence? Have you

taken on a permanent role here?" His disapproving tone put her on the defensive.

"Yes. I'd like to. Do you have an issue with that, Mr. Owens?" She met his eyes, and he looked away in surprise. He clearly didn't expect her to challenge him.

"Of course not. It's fine. I just didn't know. It's good to know, that's all."

Eliza smiled and sat at her desk. "I hope you have a lovely day, Mr. Owens."

"You as well." He backed out of the office and she breathed a sigh of relief. What a peculiar man.

"How long has Richard worked with you?" Eliza asked when her father was settled at his desk.

He thought for a moment. "A long time. I'm not really sure how many years. Maybe twenty? We work well together. I made him a limited partner a few years ago. So he has more of a stake in the business now." Her father smiled. "He deserves it, and that way, when I eventually pass, I know the company will be in good hands and still providing well for my girls."

"So, does that mean Richard is an owner, too?" His behavior made a bit more sense now to Eliza. Any changes to the business would potentially affect him.

"Partly. He gets a small percentage of the business profits each year, in the form of a year-end bonus. He still reports to me, though. This is my company." Her father sat tall in his chair and Eliza couldn't help but admire his confidence and what he had achieved.

The firm was involved with some of the biggest and

most exciting real estate projects in the city. And she was proud that her father was insisting on building affordable units for people with lower incomes. She knew it would have been easier, and more lucrative, to focus only on the higher end market.

There was quite a lot of correspondence to go through and replies to be written. Eliza also took detailed notes at the morning meeting. Every Monday, her father met with Richard and the rest of the team—the project managers on each ongoing project. They all gave status updates and discussed any challenges they were having and if the project was on track to meet the deadlines they'd set for completion.

Eliza found it all fascinating. There was so much to keep track of. Different stages of construction sometimes couldn't begin their work until another part was completed.

"Tony's frustrated. He was scheduled to start piping for the plumbing, but the framing isn't finished yet. I had to push him out to next week," Jeff, one of the project managers, explained.

Eliza's father frowned. "Why isn't the framing done?"

"Carlos and three of his crew missed three days because of the flu."

Her father nodded. "They're ok now?"

"Carlos said they'll put in extra time to try to catch us up," Jeff added.

"Good. Three days isn't too bad. What else do I need to know about?"

The meeting finished a little after noon. Eliza's father headed back into the office while Eliza tucked her notes away in her desk drawer. She'd type them up in the morning. Harry was waiting for her outside. She knew he'd arrived at noon sharp, so she didn't want to be late.

"You're off then? I'll see you tonight for dinner?" Her father smiled as Richard tapped on the door, wanting a word. Eliza waved goodbye and headed outside. Harry was leaning against the carriage, his face turned up to let the sun wash over him. His dark curls glistened in the sunlight. Eliza watched him for a moment, not wanting to interrupt. He heard her footsteps, though, and turned her way. He grinned and his whole face lit up. Eliza felt her mood brighten instantly.

"It's a gorgeous day. The sun feels good." Harry opened the door and helped her inside the carriage. Once she was settled, Eliza noticed an intriguing smell. The scent of some kind of food drifting towards her. She glanced out the window but didn't see any street vendors.

"Do you smell something?" She was curious to know what the intoxicating scent was.

"It's my mother's meat pies. I stopped in to say hello on my way here and she insisted on giving me a stack of pies. I have plenty, if you'd like to try one," he offered.

"Oh no! I don't want to take your food. Thank you though. That's very kind of you."

Harry laughed. "It's really no trouble at all. She sent me enough to practically feed the whole house. We could drive to the park and eat outside. I'm assuming you haven't had luncheon yet?"

"No. I thought I would just find something at home."

"So, it's settled then? We can be at the park, eating meat pies in less than five minutes. Just say the word."

It was tempting. As Eliza was about to graciously refuse, her stomach rumbled loudly and she laughed. "All right. If you're sure you have enough?"

A few minutes later, Harry turned into Central Park and went a short way before stopping by a shady tree and a wooden bench.

"How's this spot?" He asked.

The tree leaves rustled as a slight breeze blew and the sun shone down on the bench. It would be a warm, peaceful place to sit.

"It's lovely," Eliza said.

Harry came to a stop and jumped out and loosely tied the reins to a post by the bench. He opened her door and held out his hand to assist her. A moment later, Eliza was sitting on the bench with a half-moon shaped meat pie in her hand. The pastry was golden brown and still warm. She tentatively took a small bite, which was immediately followed by a bigger one. It was filled with chopped beef, onions, peppers and a rich brown gravy.

"This is delicious."

Harry smiled. "I'll thank my mother on your behalf. She's the best cook I know."

Harry made her laugh as they ate, telling her about his family, his siblings, and his mother. He found humor in everything and his positive attitude was contagious as he updated her on his business venture.

"It's progressing nicely. Another few months and we'll be ready to go. I've started laying the groundwork and talking to some of my father's old contacts. Some of them clearly think I'm full of it and don't mind telling me as much, but most are cautiously optimistic. They've so much as said if I really do get this thing up and running, they're interested in working with me."

"That's great, Harry." Eliza was happy for him. She had no doubt that someday, maybe even someday soon, he'd be off and running to make his dreams come true. She admired his ambition and his passion.

"Enough about me. How was your weekend? I'm sure you had all the men fighting to dance with you at that fancy party?"

Eliza smiled. "It was fun. And the opera was lovely too. Do you enjoy it?"

He nodded. "I do. I don't go often, but once a year, my mother and sisters and I all go as a family. We used to do that with my father, and we all wanted to keep the tradition going."

"How come you're not engaged yet, Harry?" Eliza knew that he was several years older and most people were married by then. If things were different—if Eliza was a ladies' maid in Manhattan—she might have had quite a crush on Harry. He was easy to talk to, and he really was quite handsome, too. He seemed to grow more attractive as the weeks went by and she got to know him better. She thought of the expectation that she would be engaged by the end of the season and sighed. It really seemed impossible. Though it was still early in the season. She supposed there might still be time yet to either meet some new people or further develop a relationship with someone she'd met already.

Harry was quiet for a long moment. "Well, that's quite the question, isn't it?"

"I'm sorry. I didn't mean to be intrusive. I'm just surprised you haven't been snapped up," she admitted.

He laughed. "Well, I think that's one of the nicest compliments I've received yet. Truthfully, I almost got engaged several years ago. Mabel was a lovely girl, and I fell fast and asked her to marry me just a few months after meeting her. But she turned me down."

"Oh no!" Eliza wondered how this Mabel could have said no to Harry.

"I was crushed. Turns out she'd taken a fancy to my friend Billy and they got engaged a month later. They have two children and, from what I hear, are quite happy."

"I'm sorry, Harry."

He smiled. "I'm long over it. Decided she did me a favor, actually. I'm not in any hurry to marry now. I want to build my fortune first, and I need my focus to be on my business."

Eliza could understand that, too. She envied whoever eventually married Harry and hoped there might be more men out there like him.

"So, what about you, then? Do you fancy anyone you've

met yet?" He grinned. "That's the goal of these affairs, I believe."

She laughed. "Yes, that is one of the main purposes. I've been informed that we are expected to meet someone 'suitable' and get engaged hopefully by the end of the season. I don't know if I can do that, though."

"No one 'suitable enough'?" Harry raised his eyebrows teasingly, but she also noticed an undercurrent of something and worried that she might have offended him. She hadn't meant anything by the word suitable, but they both knew that as the family's driver, Harry would never be considered 'suitable' in that way. It didn't seem fair. Eliza had never minded before as being a ladies' maid and serving a grand family was all she knew. Now that her place in society had changed, it was a strange adjustment. And it still felt unfair.

"Just no one that I really enjoy spending time with is what I mean."

"Right. That's important. You have to really like someone's company if you're going to get engaged. Might not be much fun otherwise." He made a face, and she laughed, glad that he'd lightened the mood and hadn't seemed to take offense.

"You do. I told my grandmother that I might not be able to make a decision that big so quickly."

Harry looked surprised. "Oh, and how did she take that?"

"Surprisingly well. She admitted that she quite enjoyed not being married, and that I was welcome to stay with the family as long as I liked—even if that meant I'd be a spinster. She suggested it might not be such a terrible thing."

Harry chuckled. "Somehow, I don't see you as a spinster. But I do agree with your grandmother. It's never a good idea to rush these things."

20

When Eliza stepped through the front door, she felt two pairs of curious eyes on her. Rose and Alice both held several invitations and looked as though they'd been in deep discussion. Alice handed Eliza a stack of envelopes, most of them the thick paper that usually indicated an invitation of some sort. "These came for you today," she said shortly, while Rose watched in silence.

"Thank you." Eliza escaped into the nearby sitting room to open her correspondence. She expected to be alone and was surprised when both Alice and Rose followed her into the room and sat on a nearby sofa. No one spoke while Eliza opened each envelope. Among them were the formal invitations from Minnie and Will for the gatherings they'd mentioned at Mrs. Astor's party. There were a few other invitations from people she either didn't know or had briefly met, and she assumed that Alice and Rose received those invitations as well.

The air in the room was decidedly chilly, so Eliza decided to take her correspondence upstairs and pen her replies alone in her room. She stood to leave and was surprised when Alice spoke again.

"Neither of us were invited to Will's event. I assume from the thickness of the envelope that he is having some kind of party? I'm sure our invitations will likely arrive tomorrow," she sniffed. It was clear that Alice simply couldn't fathom the thought that the two of them were left off the guest list if Eliza was invited.

"Will mentioned it to me at Mrs. Astor's party, actually. It's just a small gathering for people who enjoy the arts, opera especially."

Alice made a face. "Well, that sounds perfectly dreadful. I suppose Minnie's event is something similar?"

"No, hers has nothing to do with the arts. I think she wanted me to meet a few of her friends who are also interested in the business world."

"You mean they work? Like you do in father's office?" Rose asked.

Eliza nodded. "I believe so. Minnie doesn't work, but she spends a lot of time investing her money and managing those investments."

Alice yawned. "That doesn't sound very interesting, either."

Rose smiled at her sister. "I'm sure that's why we weren't invited, Alice."

"I suppose you're right."

Eliza forced a smile. "I'll see you both at dinner tonight."

Later that evening, as Miriam was helping Eliza dress for dinner, Eliza asked about Alice and Rose's mother. All she knew of Mary Redfield was that she'd died suddenly two years prior from influenza. Eliza was curious to learn more about Mary's personality and wondered if it might shed some light on Alice's and Rose's behavior. She couldn't understand why Alice was so cold towards her. Rose kept her distance too, though she at least was civil.

Miriam hesitated before answering and when she spoke, seemed to choose her words carefully. "Mary Redfield was an… interesting and often challenging woman. She was very particular and could be demanding —impatient more than anything. When she wanted some-thing, she expected it to be done immediately."

"What kind of relationship did she have with Alice and Rose? Were they close?"

"I think so. She spent most of her time with the girls. They often went out to social events while Mr. Redfield stayed home. They were quite the opposite in that way. He likes to be home. She liked to be out."

"Were they happy?" Eliza hoped so.

Miriam nodded. "As happy as most, I suppose. She was from an important family. I don't know if it was a love match or not, but their marriage brought two well-regarded families together."

Eliza thought of her mother and how she'd never had an opportunity to marry the man she loved. And he was never informed of her condition. Though Eliza wondered if that might have been worse—for her mother to actually be rejected. Because their union would not have been allowed. Eliza supposed it might have meant less heart-break to simply accept that it was impossible.

"Do either of the girls take after her?" Eliza asked.

"Rose actually looks like her. But Alice has her person-ality." A moment later she frowned. "Mrs. Redfield spoiled those girls. She denied them nothing and I've heard they grew up expecting to have their every wish granted. As you may have noticed, at times they can be a bit difficult. Well, Rose is fine. It's Alice who sometimes gets in a mood."

Eliza nodded. "I don't think she likes me very much."

"I don't think she would like any attractive woman who might take the attention away from her. To her, you are competition. It's a shame, really."

Eliza couldn't agree more. "It is a shame. I have no desire to compete with Alice. I hoped we could all be friends."

"Give it time. Maybe someday things will be different."

That Thursday evening, Harry drove Eliza to Minnie's house. It wasn't terribly far, she'd considered walking, but Miriam advised against it.

"It's not wise for a young woman to be walking alone after dark. One can't be too careful. And your grand-mother would never allow it." Miriam looked as though she was about to say something else and bit her tongue. It took Eliza a moment to realize what she'd been about to say. It would reflect poorly on Miriam if Eliza set off alone. Eliza didn't want to risk Miriam getting into trouble, and she also recognized good advice when she heard it.

The ride to Minnie's took less than ten minutes. Eliza chatted easily with Harry as they drove. He knew of Minnie and shared his insights with her.

"I don't know her personally, but a friend works for them and said Miss Minnie is impressive. He's a footman, so he overhears their dinner conversations and not to gossip of course, but he was fascinated by the discussions she has with her husband. He said she knows as much about the world of business as her husband does."

Eliza wasn't surprised to hear it. "She's very interested in banking and investing."

"Maybe she'll teach you a thing or two. If that interests you?"

"It does actually." It was far more intriguing to Eliza than planning what dress to wear for one of the many upcoming functions she was required to attend.

"I thought it might, since you seem to enjoy going into the office with your uncle," Harry said as they pulled up to a grand house. "Here we are."

He said he'd be back to collect her in two hours, which was how long Miriam had suggested the evening would last.

Eliza made her way to the front door and before she could knock, the door swung open and Minnie pulled her in for a welcome hug.

"I happened to look out the window and saw your carriage pull up. I'm so glad you're here. Come in and I'll show you around. The others are still arriving."

Minnie led Eliza into a large drawing room. There were two other young women seated on a green velvet upholstered sofa. They were both sipping what looked like wine, or maybe champagne. Minnie introduced Eliza to them as a footman came over to offer a glass of champagne. Eliza took one from his silver tray and sat next to Minnie on a matching sofa that faced the other two women. They both looked to be about Eliza's age, or maybe a little older, and they were both married.

Two more women arrived soon after, also close to her age and also both married. Eliza felt a twinge of worry as she realized if she wasn't engaged by the end of the season —she really was going to be the odd one out.

She learned over dinner, though, that one of the women was already a widow.

"How are you doing?" Minnie asked when Helen mentioned that it was the one-year anniversary of her husband's death and that they'd only been married for five years.

Helen was blond and slight and Eliza realized she was a few years older than she'd first guessed.

"I'm all right. It is strange to think it has been a year already. Though in some ways it feels like Fred has been gone much longer. I still miss him terribly. But it is getting easier. Except when a holiday or an anniversary comes and then it hurts." She smiled sadly. "I was grateful for your invitation and for the opportunity to be busy on this date."

Eliza couldn't imagine how painful it must be to lose a husband at such a young age. They'd only just started their life together. She wondered what had happened, but didn't want to ask. Helen looked her way and seemed to sense the unspoken question.

"It was a hunting accident. Someone meant to shoot a deer and got Fred instead."

"I'm so sorry," Eliza said.

Helen smiled slightly. "Thank you. I'm doing well now, thanks to everyone's support. I always look forward to these gatherings with just the girls." She looked around the room. "I do not miss the regular season events. Though I suppose it's almost time to start attending those again. Or people will talk."

"Let them talk!" Minnie exclaimed and then added more gently, "I really don't think they will, though. No one would mind if you sat this season out."

"Is your social life as busy when you're married?" Eliza asked. That would be one advantage of getting married if attendance at the endless parade of teas, dinners and balls slowed. Not that she minded them entirely. But there were just so many—it was a bit exhausting.

Minnie grinned. "I attend as few as possible. There are some we must make an appearance at, but I manage to miss most of them. I just send a lovely note of regrets that we're not available that evening. Everyone assumes we are going elsewhere—so it works out perfectly. Ted is actually more of the social butterfly than I am. I'd miss almost all of them if I could, but he insists on dragging me out to a few. It is good for his business, so I have to think of that."

The others all nodded in agreement.

"What if one doesn't marry?" Eliza asked.

The others all exchanged glances and then Minnie asked, "Do you mean ever?"

"I really don't know. I've always assumed, of course, that some day I will marry. But I worry a bit that an engagement is expected to happen by the end of this season. What if it doesn't?"

The others all laughed, as if the idea was ridiculous. "I'm sure you'll have your pick of offers," Minnie assured her.

"But what if I don't want to marry any of them? What if I don't fall in love that fast?"

Once again, glances were exchanged around the table.

"I wasn't sure that I was fully in love with my Fred, but I enjoyed spending time with him and he was already in love with me, so I agreed to marry him," Helen said. "And it wasn't long before I was madly in love with him. I think that's how it was for most of us."

The others nodded. "I definitely wasn't in love with Ted," Minnie said. "But I found him the least annoying and so far, it has worked out fine."

The others all laughed, including Eliza, but she wondered about her friend's marriage. Minnie seemed happy enough, but Eliza wanted more—she wanted to be fully in love before agreeing to marry. But maybe that wasn't realistic?

"But to answer your question—if you don't marry this season, you'll start over next season, though it may be more difficult for you. People will wonder why you didn't marry—and there will be a new crop of young girls for the men to choose from."

Eliza shuddered at the thought of going through it all again.

Minnie laughed. "It's a horrid thought, isn't it? That's why it's best to choose someone, if you can. Get that over with, so you can move on to the next phase of your life."

"What if someone still doesn't marry, though? They become a spinster, but what does that actually mean?" Eliza asked.

"If a girl goes too long, say another full season or so and doesn't marry, then her prospects are truly limited. Society doesn't really know what to do with an unmarried woman —especially if it's the woman's choice. It will be much more difficult if she changes her mind and decides she wanted to find a husband at a later date," Minnie cautioned.

"Are you not interested in marriage?" Helen asked.

"It's not that. It's only that I just arrived here and am still settling in. It feels fast, that's all." Eliza smiled to assure them that she wasn't actively desiring to be a spinster. She really was just curious what it would mean if she didn't rush to get engaged in the next few months. It felt over-whelmingly fast.

"Well, I don't think it would be the end of the world if you needed another year. You're new here after all," Minnie said reassuringly.

"Thank you. It was also a comment my grandmother made—she said she quite enjoyed her independence after my grandfather passed. She missed him, of course, but she said it is quite lovely to come and go as she pleases and to do whatever she likes."

Minnie grinned. "We have that too, though. My husband allows me to spend time and money how I choose. I was already investing long before we met and I told him I intended to continue after we married and if that was going to be a problem, then we shouldn't marry."

The others all nodded in agreement, much to Eliza's surprise.

"We don't all invest the way that Minnie does," Helen explained. "Fred wasn't keen on that. He didn't trust it. But he did allow me to write for the local paper and I still love doing that. Now that he's gone, I have started doing a little investing, too." She glanced at Minnie. "I always paid attention even though I wasn't doing it myself. I learned a lot by just listening."

"And she's doing great now," Minnie said proudly.

Once dinner was finished, they adjourned to the drawing room for coffee and Minnie began the discussion. They went around the room and shared how their invest-ments had done in the month since they'd last met and shared what they were thinking of doing next. Eliza found it all fascinating to listen to—especially when it was Minnie's turn. She let the others go first and then filled them in on her many investments and explained her overall strategy to Eliza.

"I invest in some stocks, but my focus is real estate and railroads. I don't build, as that is not my area of expertise, but I do buy, rent and hold. I'm considering selling a block of land I've held for some time now. It's in an area that is seeing quite a bit of development lately and I imagine some of those builders may be interested in acquiring it. She mentioned the address and Eliza mentally pictured it and realized it was on the same street, just a block away from her father's newest development project—the one that would have affordable housing.

"Do you have anyone in mind to sell it to?" Eliza asked.

"No, not yet. I've only just thought it might be time to look into it." Her eyes lit up. "Why do you ask? Do you think your uncle could be interested?"

Eliza smiled. "Possibly. I don't know his plans for acquiring more property this year, but I think he may like that location."

"Tell him it's a full block. He could do a lot with that."

"I'll tell him."

The evening flew by and before she knew it, a tall grandfather clock chimed that three hours had passed. It seemed to be a signal—everyone moved to leave and thanked Minnie for a wonderful evening.

"Did you enjoy yourself?" Minnie asked as she walked

PAMELA KELLEY

Eliza to the front door. "I hope the business talk wasn't too boring?" Her eyes twinkled though, and Eliza laughed.

"No, not at all. It was wonderful. I learned so much. Thank you for including me."

Minnie looked pleased to hear it. "I thought you might enjoy this group. We gather once a month, usually at my house. I hope you can join us again."

"I look forward to it."

Harry was waiting for her and jumped out to open the door for Eliza as she approached the carriage. Once she was settled in the back seat, he drove off and asked if she'd had an enjoyable evening. Eliza smiled to herself in the darkness. Her head was positively spinning with all the information she'd received and she planned to find her notebook as soon as she undressed to write down as much as she could remember from the various conversations. And she would ask her father about that land in the morning.

"It was a magical evening. They are lovely women. We had such an interesting discussion—and it wasn't what you'd expect."

"Really? What did you discuss?"

"Mostly finance, investments, and real estate. I learned a lot. Minnie has been investing for years and the others are following in her footsteps. It's exciting."

"That does sound interesting. I'm starting to learn about those things myself. I know a bit about business—but not the investing part." He chuckled. "I need money to invest first for that."

Eliza laughed too. "You will have it someday, Harry. I have no doubt." She admired his passion for wanting to start his own business.

"Thank you. I'm going to give it my all. Hopefully, very soon."

21

*E*liza waited until she was in the office the next morning to mention Minnie's land to her father. He was immediately intrigued.

"She owns that entire block? That's so close to our new project. I'd love to get my hands on that land. You're sure it's all available?"

Eliza nodded. "Yes, she said she's ready to see about selling it. She's owned it for a number of years."

"Could you draft a letter to her today asking for a meeting? I'd like to talk to her before she speaks with anyone else."

"I'll get the letter out today." Eliza was pleased that her father seemed excited about the property. It made sense to her that more buildings in that area would be of interest to him. She loved sitting in their meetings and was soaking up so much information just by taking notes, which she typed up and gave to her father each week for his records.

Later that morning, during their weekly planning meeting with the rest of the team, her father mentioned the property.

"I've learned that there might be a full block available almost next to our existing project. I am going to be aggressive about trying to acquire this property. I'm sure you all realize the potential there?"

Everyone around the table nodded. Richard frowned. "I've asked after that property once a year and there's never been interest in selling. It was just a few months ago when I last inquired. How did you hear that it was available?"

Eliza's father looked her way and smiled. "Eliza brought it to my attention."

"Eliza did? Really?" Richard sounded incredulous at the very thought of it.

Her father chuckled. "She's friends with the owner, Minnie Greene."

Richard looked confused. "Minnie is the owner? I assumed it was her husband, Ted. That's who I've addressed all my inquiries to."

"Perhaps the properties are under his name?" Her father suggested.

"I believe she said that they are," Eliza interjected and smiled. "But they are Minnie's and she happened to mention that she is considering selling, so of course I thought there might be interest here—given the proximity to the other project."

Her father beamed at her with pride while Richard still looked confused and annoyed.

PAMELA KELLEY

"Minnie has the say on selling those properties? Is that what you are saying?" He asked.

"Yes, that is correct," Eliza confirmed.

"We're getting a letter off today asking for a meeting to discuss. Hopefully, we'll come to an agreement on price and move forward to acquire the land," her father said.

The rest of the morning went by quickly. Eliza typed up her notes and handled all the correspondence, including a letter to Minnie.

"I can actually give this to Minnie personally if you like? I'll be seeing her this afternoon," Eliza said as she readied to leave for the day.

"If you could, I'd appreciate it. The sooner the better. And thank you again for bringing this to my attention. I'm so pleased that you are taking to the business and realized how valuable that particular address could be for us."

Eliza smiled. "I'm enjoying it. I find it all quite fascinating."

Eliza was still smiling as she walked outside, holding the letter for Minnie as she climbed into the carriage.

"Did you have a good day?" Harry asked as they drove off. "You look particularly happy."

"I did actually." She filled Harry in on Minnie's land and that they were eager to acquire it.

"Actually, instead of going home, would it be possible to bring me to the Chemical Bank? I told Minnie that I would meet her there when I finished work for the day."

"Of course. How long do you expect to be? I can wait for you or come back a bit later."

"I'm not sure exactly. Maybe a half hour or an hour? I hate to keep you waiting."

"Not to worry. I'll check back in a half hour and if you're not ready then, I'll come back."

Eliza made her way into the bank and felt a bit intimidated as everywhere she looked, she saw men in dark suits. There wasn't a woman in sight. She gripped her purse tightly—it held her life savings, all of her earnings from working as a ladies' maid. She stood still for a moment before walking to the counter and tentatively asked if Minnie was there. Perhaps she'd misunderstood and was meant to meet her at her house.

But at the mention of Minnie's name, the bank teller smiled. "Mrs. Greene has her own office. I will show you where it is." He came out from behind the counter and led Eliza around the corner and down a hallway to a small office. The door was ajar slightly and through it, Eliza could see Minnie sitting behind a desk, frowning at a piece of paper full of handwritten numbers. A stack of newspapers was by her side. She looked up and smiled when she saw Eliza.

"You found me! Come on in and have a seat. Thanks ever so much, Paul, for bringing her to me."

"Of course. You ladies have a nice afternoon." Paul disappeared and Eliza entered the room and sat across from Minnie. For the next forty-five minutes, Minnie walked her through how she did her research and which stocks she liked at the moment. Eliza brought her notebook and wrote feverishly, trying to keep up with everything that Minnie shared with her. She was so intent on what she was learning that she almost forgot to give Minnie her father's letter. She pulled it out of her purse and set it on the desk.

"I mentioned your property to my uncle this morning, and he would like to set a meeting with you to discuss it."

A look of surprise flashed across Minnie's face, followed by a big smile. "Excellent. I didn't expect anything would happen so quickly. Thank you for talking to him so soon. I can meet with him at his convenience."

Eliza thought for a moment. She'd looked over her father's appointments for the week. "Could you come by the office tomorrow at eleven? He's free then, if that works for you."

Minnie nodded. "I'll be there. Now, let's focus on you. These are the two stocks I'd suggest. Let's go get an account open for you. That should only take a few minutes."

Eliza followed Minnie back to the counter, and Paul opened an account for her. Minnie explained how she could withdraw the funds to purchase stocks. Once everything was set, Eliza thanked her before heading outside to meet Harry.

"It's my pleasure. And Eliza, I'm here every day, all afternoon. I usually arrive at eleven once everything is in order at home. And I stay until the bank closes at four. Come by anytime and I'm happy to talk about what I'm seeing in the market. I'd love it, actually." Her passion was contagious.

"I definitely will. Thank you so much!"

22

TWO MONTHS LATER

"*E*liza, what do you think of this painting?" Will drew her attention to his newest acquisition. They were at his home on a Thursday evening for one of his salon gatherings. Eliza had loved the first one and was now a regular attendee. She'd enjoyed meeting Will's friends. Aside from his sister, Olivia, the others were mostly male and married. The few single ones were all engaged now, except for Will, though Eliza had begun to sense from the looks others gave the two of them whenever they were together, that they were hoping Will might propose to her soon. Eliza wasn't sure how she felt about that.

She liked Will quite a lot. She loved spending time with him, but as yet, she hadn't felt the romantic spark she assumed one should feel. It surprised her because Will was by far the most handsome man she'd ever met. The closest she'd come to feeling anything remotely like a spark was actually with Harry. Once or twice, when they'd been deep in conversation about something, she'd felt a shift in the air. But it vanished so quickly that she'd wondered if she'd imagined it. Harry had never been anything but respectful towards her. And she knew a romance with him was unfortunately out of the question.

"It's quite lovely. Breathtaking, even." It was an oil painting of two figures standing by a bench in Central Park and the whole top half of the painting had vividly-colored leaves everywhere—in the trees, and swirling in the air, falling towards the ground. The figures were blurred, so it was impossible to make out any details, but they were standing close together and the overall feeling was romantic. The painting looked lit up from within—the use of color on the leaves and sunlight coming through the trees was extraordinary. And the colors were so vibrant.

"Thank you. The moment I saw it, I knew I had to have it. There's a matching painting of a different area of the park that might compliment it. What do you think? Should I get that one too?"

"If it's anything like this one, then I would say yes. They'll both look beautiful in this room." They were standing in Will's library, which was a large room lined with bookcases that were almost completely full of leather-bound books with gilded gold lettering. A dark pine desk sat in a corner, with two large leather armchairs facing a roaring fire that cast an inviting glow on the rest of the room.

"There's something I'd like to discuss with you," Will began. His face and tone shifted, and he suddenly sounded quite serious. Eliza felt an immediate sense of dread as to what might be coming. And she realized she probably shouldn't be feeling that way if, in fact, he was about to propose.

"Excuse me, sir. Dinner is ready, if you'd like to head into the dining room." They were interrupted by one of his footmen, who had silently glided over to make the announcement. His best friend Marcus was right behind the footman and smiled big when he saw them both. "I just poked my head in the kitchen and caught a glimpse of the prime rib. Looks like you've outdone yourself tonight, my friend."

For a moment, Will looked frozen and Eliza sensed he was debating whether to have this conversation now or after dinner. The footman left, but Marcus stayed standing nearby, which made the decision for Will.

"We can talk after dinner. Let's go eat. Cook does a marvelous job with Prime Rib. I hope you're hungry?"

Eliza smiled. "Always. It sounds delicious." She followed them into the dining room and they joined the others. There were twelve people in the group that evening and Eliza now felt that she could call them all friends. Will's sister, Olivia, was lovely and was seated on Eliza's left. Will was on her right.

Dinner was lively as they all discussed a new show that

had recently opened at the Opera House. There was also a riveting discussion of a Henry James novel, *The Bostonians*.

"James obviously can't stand anyone from Boston," Marcus said.

"It's entirely unfair," his friend, Alan, agreed.

"You have to admit, though, the satire is on point?" Will said, and everyone nodded.

"I thought it was fantastic," Olivia said.

"Of course you did—you loved the inherent feminism," Will said and laughed.

"You're right. It delved quite a bit into politics and I think was quite accurate," Olivia agreed.

Once everyone finished dessert, they took their after-dinner drinks—a good bourbon for the men and coffee for the women—into the drawing room. Once Eliza had joined them for an after-dinner cocktail instead of the coffee and had regretted it the next day when she woke with a splitting headache. There was always a fair amount of wine flowing during these dinners and she'd learned that was quite enough for her. She didn't know how the men managed. Unless they just didn't mind feeling horrible the next day. She'd asked Olivia about it once.

"Isn't your brother miserable in the morning?"

Olivia had laughed. "No. I think he's quite used to it. Men can handle more alcohol, I suppose. Like you, I prefer coffee, too."

They played charades for an hour or so after dinner, and it was great fun. It always was, but eventually there were a few yawns and people began to leave. Eliza went to join them as she was tired, too, but Will caught her eye and shook his head—silently communicating that he wanted her to stay.

Once everyone left, he led Eliza back to his library and motioned for her to sit in one of the cozy leather chairs that faced the fireplace. He sat on the other and turned her way.

"I wanted you to stay because I have something important to discuss with you," he began.

Eliza nodded and held her breath for a moment, bracing herself.

"I really like you, Eliza. We have so many shared interests and I think we get along quite well. As you know, it's expected that we both find partners this season. There's quite a lot of pressure to do so. Because we get on so well, I'd like to propose that we marry. But it won't be a typical arrangement. I want to be quite clear with you on that as it wouldn't be fair otherwise—and I completely understand if this doesn't suit you. I do ask, however, for your discretion —that you keep this conversation private."

Eliza felt quite confused. This wasn't what she'd ever envisioned for a proposal. Though she didn't feel romantically inclined towards Will, she was surprised that he didn't speak at all of romance, but instead of how well they got on, how they shared similar interests. He didn't mention finding her beautiful or look at her with any hint of desire. She felt a flash of annoyance and realized how hypocritical that was because she didn't feel that way either. She waited for him to continue.

"If we marry, I won't expect anything from you other than friendship. But to all appearances, we will be man and wife." He paused and waited for her reaction.

Eliza felt even more confused. "I don't understand."

He took a deep breath. "I have other interests in that regard. Which is why it is so important for me to marry and to appear to have a normal marriage. My lifestyle is not accepted, unfortunately. I don't know that it ever will be. And the longer I stay unmarried, the more people may start to question why."

"I see." And finally, it all made sense. Now she understood the unusually close friendship Will had with Marcus. Now the looks between them that she hadn't thought anything of before took on a different meaning.

"Is it Marcus?" Maybe it was someone else and Marcus really was just his good friend—he was married, after all. She tried to make sense of it.

Will nodded. "For nearly five years now."

"I wasn't sure as he's married."

"In name only. The arrangement works for Harriet."

"Oh. I see. Why did you think it might work for me?"

"I wasn't sure. I hoped—like I said, I really do like you, Eliza. We could have great fun together as the friends that we are. You don't seem keen on anyone else and you're very interested in business. It would be a way of being independent and still very accepted in society. If that matters to you?"

"I don't know how much it matters." She stood and faced Will. "I'll keep your secret, but I can't marry you. If I marry, and it doesn't look like that will happen this season or anytime soon, but if I do, it will only be for love. If I end up a spinster, so be it."

Will stood and grinned. "I admire that. I'm sorry the proposal doesn't work for you. I still need to find someone that will take me on, but I understand why you won't. Are we still friends? I hope I haven't offended you?"

Eliza smiled. "You couldn't, possibly. I am honored that you asked, and that you were honest with me. I know not everyone would be."

Will frowned. "I know there are people who will say whatever they need to get what they want. But I couldn't imagine doing that to a friend. And I do consider you one of my best friends, Eliza. I hope that won't ever change."

"I feel the same."

Will pulled her in for a hug. "I'll walk you outside."

Harry waited outside in the carriage and once Eliza was settled and they were on their way, he asked how the evening had gone.

"It was memorable. One never knows what to expect at one of Will's parties, and he outdid himself this time. How are things with you?"

"Well, I have some news. I put in my notice today. The funding came in and two weeks from now I'll be opening the doors of Ford Clothing.

Eliza felt a mix of joy and disappointment. She hated the thought of Harry leaving, though she'd known for months that the day was coming.

"That's the best news, Harry. The very best. You know, of course, that you'll be missed terribly? I'll miss you."

"I'll miss you all too—you especially. But if it's okay, I'll keep in touch, and let you know how things are going?"

"I'd really love that."

23

"You're quiet tonight, Miss Eliza. Was it a fun time?" Miriam asked as she helped Eliza undress.

"It's always a fun time at Will's gatherings. I think I'm just tired." Eliza was dying to confide in Miriam, but she didn't dare. She'd given Will her word that she would be discreet. The proposal had been so unexpected. She'd never suspected that there was anything more between Will and Marcus than friendship. And why would she? Marcus was happily married. Or so it seemed. And so she understood why Will wished for a similar arrangement. She knew everyone would have approved of the match and thought she'd done well to capture the season's most eligible bachelor.

Instead, it looked as though she might be heading toward being a spinster after all. There was no one else who appealed to her. Nick liked to flirt with her, but he flirted with everyone, and Eliza didn't feel romantically drawn toward him either. And she knew Alice wanted him for herself. She hoped that would work out because it wouldn't be an awful thing for Alice to move out. Eliza was tired of her frosty attitude, which hadn't thawed in the slightest.

"How are you feeling, Miriam?" Miriam was just starting to show a little—her waist was slightly thicker and Eliza guessed she might have a bit of a bump, but for now, it was hidden under her skirts.

"I'm feeling very well. Thank you for asking. I'm not as tired as I used to be, though I have had some odd cravings lately."

Eliza smiled. "What do you crave?"

"Vanilla ice cream and pickles—together. Isn't that the strangest thing? Mrs. Shelby told me it was quite normal, though. She's made sure to keep both in stock."

Eliza laughed. "She takes good care of you."

"She does. I'm very lucky."

"Harry put his notice in today," Eliza said.

"I heard. He'll be missed. It's a fantastic opportunity for him. The way he talks about that business—he can see it doing well. I expect he'll be a huge success."

"I believe you are right. I hope so."

Two days later, there was another ball to attend. This time it was Nick's family hosting at their relatives' home, where they spent the season. It was a lovely event, similar to the many others Eliza had attended. After a while, they all sort of blurred together. There was a long, sumptuous dinner with many courses and different wines throughout, followed by hours of dancing.

Eliza noticed that Alice was frowning more than usual. She supposed it was because Nick wasn't by her side as much as she'd like. He was helping his family to host and, as such, had to be sure to mingle and speak with all the guests. Eventually, he made his way to Eliza.

"I saved the best for last," he teased. "Now we can relax and chat a bit before the next dance. We haven't really talked for ages. What is new with you?" He looked as though he expected her to share some juicy gossip, but she just laughed.

"Not a thing. I'm afraid my life is not that exciting."

He raised his eyebrows. "No? I thought perhaps you might have a big announcement. The rumor mill has been swirling that Will was going to propose a few days ago."

Eliza shouldn't have been surprised that the rumor spread, but she was. "That's not going to happen," she said quickly.

"So, he did propose then? But you said no?"

Eliza hesitated before answering, but decided it was best to be truthful without sharing all the details. "He did propose, and he's a lovely person, but I had to decline because I'm not in love with him. He is one of my dearest friends, though."

"It would be quite a match. You're sure about this? I assumed you'd say yes, and that you were off the market." A wide smile spread across his face as he realized Eliza was very much available. She felt someone's eyes upon her and turned to see Alice shooting daggers her way. Eliza shivered and was about to walk away when the band began playing a new song and Nick held out his hand.

"We haven't danced yet."

It would be impossibly rude to refuse the request, so Eliza put her hand in his and he pulled her into his arms and whirled her around the dance floor. Alice was dancing with someone else now, but every time they passed her, Alice's icy glare spoke volumes. Eliza needed Nick to bring his focus back to Alice.

"Doesn't Alice look lovely tonight? That pale blue is her best color."

Nick smiled when he saw Alice glide by. "She is a beautiful girl," he agreed.

But two seconds later, his attention was back on Eliza. "You'll have to come to one of our summer parties in Newport. Our relatives have one of the original summer cottages." He chuckled. "I find it amusing that they call them that as they really are quite grand mansions."

"So, I've heard."

He looked up in surprise. "You've never been to Newport? It's quite exceptional. All the best families summer there. You must come."

Eliza nodded, but her smile faded as Alice danced by again and seeing her frosty glare so close made Eliza shiver. "I'm sure Alice would love to go to Newport."

"I'm sure she would. She's been there before, though. There's nothing like experiencing Newport for the first time."

The music slowed and Eliza felt the urge to escape—to get as far away from Nick and Alice as possible. "Thank you for the dance. If you could excuse me, I'm suddenly not feeling very well."

She found Rose and told her that she was going to have Harry bring her home, as she was feeling a bit poorly.

"I'll have him come back, so you can stay as long as you like."

Rose nodded. "I hope you feel better." She glanced at the dance floor where Alice and Will glided by and Alice finally looked happy. "I don't think Alice is in any hurry to leave."

The next morning, Eliza's grandmother surprised her by joining Eliza and her father at breakfast. She was dressed and looked ready to go out.

"Where are you off to today?" Her father asked.

Her grandmother nodded as Colin held the carafe of coffee over her cup. He poured and added a splash of heavy cream, the way she liked it. She took a small sip before answering.

"A telegram came yesterday in the late afternoon."

Eliza knew that her father had a business dinner the evening before, so likely hadn't seen her grandmother until this morning.

"What's wrong? Is it Enid?" Her father asked.

Her grandmother nodded and her eyes grew damp. She took a deep breath before speaking. "She's taken a turn for the worse. My niece wrote and suggested that I come straight away if I wanted to see her before... well, you know."

"I'm so sorry. Of course you must go. Shall I go with you?" He offered.

Her grandmother shook her head. "No, but thank you. I know you're busy. She's my only sister, so I don't want to rush back. I want to stay with her for as long as I can."

"I'm so sorry," Eliza said. She didn't know what else to say.

"There's a ship leaving today?" Her father asked.

"Yes, at eleven this morning. I want to go early as I'll need to purchase a ticket."

"I'll let Harry know when he drives us into the office. He'll come right back for you and you can leave whenever you like."

"Thank you, dear. I'll send word once I'm settled and let you know when I'll be returning."

Her father nodded, then grimaced and held a hand over his stomach.

"What is it Ward? You've gone a bit pale?" His mother asked.

He was quiet for a moment, then smiled at both of them. "It's nothing, just a bit of indigestion. I may have had one too many slices of bacon with my eggs."

Eliza hugged her grandmother goodbye when they left for the office. "Have a safe crossing and again, I am so sorry about your sister."

Her grandmother smiled sadly. "Thank you, dear. Take good care of Ward while I'm gone—he works too hard."

"I'll keep a close eye on him," Eliza promised.

Eliza noticed for the next few days that her father seemed to be having increasingly bad indigestion. At dinner several nights later, he turned pale again not long after eating a heavy meal of steak and creamed spinach washed down with several glasses of a rich cabernet. He put his hand to his chest and Eliza felt a twinge of alarm.

"Are you feeling ill? Shall we ring the doctor?"

Alice and Rose glanced up from their desserts. Rose seemed concerned too, while Alice shook her head.

"He looks fine to me," she said and then addressed her father directly, "Are you feeling sickly?"

He smiled wanly. "I think it's just indigestion and a bit of chest pain. It's probably just gas. This was a heavy meal and I may have over-indulged. I'll be fine. No need to call the doctor."

"Are you sure? It's no trouble. Maybe you should be looked at," Eliza insisted.

"Don't fuss, Eliza, he said he's fine," Alice snapped.

Rose looked concerned, though. "I agree with Eliza, father. It's no trouble to call the doctor. You don't look well."

Her father shook his head. "No, I'll be fine. It's really just a bit of indigestion. It will pass. If I still don't feel well tomorrow, I will think about contacting the doctor. But I'm sure that won't be necessary."

Eliza could see that his mind was made up, but she was still worried. He really didn't seem himself. She knew he'd eaten a heavy meal though—they all had. Mrs. Shelby had outdone herself with a decadent steak entrée, a delicious thick sirloin smothered in a mushroom, onion, butter, and red-wine reduction sauce. The creamed spinach was so good too—made with heavy cream, butter and a touch of cheese. It was a combination that could bring on indigestion if one over-indulged. Eliza had enjoyed every bite, but was glad that she'd only eaten a small amount. She hoped that her father would feel better in the morning.

Eliza was the first one down to breakfast the next day, which was a first. Her father was always there ahead of her and was usually on his second cup of coffee when Eliza arrived.

"Good morning, Miss Eliza," Colin said. "Your usual coffee, eggs, and toast?"

"Yes, please, Colin. Thank you."

He filled her coffee cup and turned to go.

"Colin, my uncle hasn't been down at all yet?" It really wasn't like him.

"No sign of him. I'm sure he'll be along any moment."

Eliza sipped her coffee and glanced at the morning paper, which was waiting on the table for her father. He always read it first and by the time Eliza sat down, he pushed it her way. She just glanced at the headlines. Colin returned a few minutes later with her plate of scrambled eggs and buttered toast. There still no sign of her father, and Eliza was getting worried. Maybe he was feeling too ill to come down.

"Colin, would you mind checking on my uncle? Maybe

he'd like something brought to his room. He wasn't feeling well last night at dinner."

"Of course. I'll go right now."

He headed upstairs and Eliza took a small bite of eggs and nibbled on a piece of toast. She wasn't very hungry. Her appetite disappeared completely when Colin returned to the room five minutes later, looking upset and nervous.

"What is it, Colin? Is my uncle feeling ill?"

"I'm so sorry, Miss Eliza. I thought he was sleeping, and I didn't want to disturb him, but he seemed so still that I wanted to make sure he was ok, that he was still breathing. I checked his pulse and I'm just so sorry. He passed in his sleep, I'm afraid. I've alerted Canning. He'll know what to do."

Eliza stood. "I need to see him. He must just be sleeping. He wasn't feeling well, like I said."

"I'm so sorry," Colin said again.

Eliza ran upstairs to her father's room. Canning was already there, leaning over him.

"He's just asleep, right?" Eliza said desperately.

Canning looked up and his eyes were damp. He shook his head. "He's not sleeping. I'm so very sorry."

Eliza ran to her father and felt his cheek. It was cool. She put her hand on his chest and it was still. There was no steady rise and fall. He was gone.

"I don't understand it. He didn't feel well at dinner, but he said it was just indigestion. It happened a few days ago, too."

"It may have been a heart attack. He passed peacefully

in his sleep," Canning said. "I'll call the funeral home to come and get him. I'll tell the girls as well and let them say their goodbyes before they come to collect him. Shall I leave you alone with him for a moment?"

Eliza nodded. The tears fell hard and fast and she tried to make sense of the fact that her father was gone—dead.

Once Canning and Colin left the room, Eliza threw her arms around her father's neck and sobbed uncontrollably. "How could you leave me?" She whispered. "I only just found you." They'd only had a few months together, and she was so enjoying getting to know him. Now she was all alone again. She still had her grandmother, of course, but it wasn't the same. And she was gone now too.

"I'm going to miss you so much," she told him softly and then turned at the sound of footsteps coming toward the door. It was Rose and Alice. Both were confused and still half-asleep. They looked taken aback when they saw Eliza's tear-stained face.

"It's true then? He really died in his sleep?" Alice asked.

"We should have insisted on calling the doctor!" Rose cried and ran over to her father.

Eliza nodded at both of them. "I'm so sorry. I can't believe he's gone. I'll leave you alone with him."

Everything was a blur after that. Canning took charge and less than an hour later, three men came for her father. They carefully carried him out and Eliza dissolved in a puddle of tears again. She'd thought she was all cried out, but there was an endless reserve of tears it seemed and she felt like she could cry forever. It was so unfair that she'd only just recently met her father and now he was gone.

She went to her room after the men left with her father and she sat at her small table and stared out the window. It didn't seem real. A few minutes later, Miriam knocked on the door lightly and entered, carrying a tray of hot tea and a plate of toasted raisin bread and butter. "I'm so, so sorry for your loss. Mrs. Shelby sends her condolences as well. She thought you might like some tea. And she said you hardly touched your breakfast."

"Thank you and please thank her for me as well."

Miriam sat the tray on the table. Eliza just stared at the toast and tea. Miriam looked near tears herself and Eliza could tell she was worried about her. Miriam took a step towards the door. "I'll check on you a bit later. If you need anything at all, just ring."

he week following her father's death was painfully sad, and the days were intolerably long. Eliza wasn't sure what to do with herself. She felt adrift and very alone. She missed her father, and she also missed the routine of going into the office with him. She hadn't been in the office since his death. She'd checked with Canning to see if she should go in and notify everyone of her father's death, but Canning said he'd already taken care of it. She was both relieved and sad at the same time. It would have been too painful to go there without her father—to see his office, empty.

But it also left her with little to do. As the family was officially in mourning. Mrs. Smith contacted their grandmother's favorite dressmaker to make proper black dresses for all of them. There would be no more attending teas, balls, or any social events for several months. Alice was not happy about this, and vented her frustration more than once at dinner.

"This is so unfair. I was so looking forward to the Forager Ball this weekend. Nick will be there, and I was hoping to spend more time with him."

"Is that really all you're concerned about? We just lost our father," Rose said shortly. It was the first time Eliza heard her use a sharp tone with her sister. And she didn't blame her. Alice really was a selfish girl.

Eliza found that she still had no appetite. Food wasn't appealing, and she didn't want to spend another moment in Alice's company.

"If you'd both excuse me, I'm going to retire to my room."

"But you've barely touched your dinner," Rose said. "Are you not feeling well?"

"I'm just not hungry. I'll see you both tomorrow."

Eliza went to bed early and woke early the next morning and decided that she was going to have a busy day. She dressed and went downstairs and ate breakfast alone. She tried not to look at the empty chair where her father usually sat. She ate slowly and read the entire copy of the newspaper, which Colin had set on the table, as usual, but this time he placed it by Eliza's seat. When Eliza finished eating and reading the paper, she went for a walk and, at a little after eleven, she asked Harry to bring her to Chemical Bank. She wanted to visit with Minnie and she was curious how her two stocks were doing.

She'd seen Harry several times since her father passed,

and he'd offered his condolences. He asked after her well-being as soon as they set off toward the bank.

"How are you doing? I know it's a hard time."

Eliza had thought she was doing a bit better, but his kind words and caring tone brought her emotions to the surface again and she dabbed at her eyes with a soft linen handkerchief.

"I really am doing better. It was just so sudden, so unexpected. I miss him," she admitted.

"Of course you do. He was a good man."

They rode along in silence for a few minutes, and then Eliza realized the date.

"Harry, I think today is your last day with us? We really will miss you."

"It is. It has come up fast. I feel badly leaving you all, but I've been training Colin and he'll do a fine job with the driving."

"I'm sure he will. Miriam said he's excited to move into the new role. I'm excited for you, Harry, I really am. I'll miss seeing you though." She smiled as she remembered getting off the ship and seeing Harry waiting for her. "You're the first person I met when I arrived here."

"Maybe when I'm a big success, our paths will cross again—you'll come shop in my department store." He sounded both teasing and confident at the same time, and it made Eliza smile.

"I look forward to that." It seemed a very long time off though, and the thought of not seeing Harry again made her feel more sad than she already was. She sighed as he pulled up to the front door of the bank.

"Here we are then. How long do you think you'll be?"

She thought for a moment. "Maybe an hour. It will be nice to visit with Minnie for a bit. I thought after that, I'd have you drop me off in the shopping district."

"Of course. Are you after anything in particular?"

"Nothing at all. I just thought it might be fun to do some window shopping. I have a big empty afternoon ahead of me," she admitted.

"I'm not needed until later this afternoon. If you like, I could walk around with you and show you my new factory. Everything is there now. I'll be opening bright and early tomorrow morning. Or I could just drop you and come back later if you'd rather be alone."

Eliza was tired of being alone. It had been a very lonely week. "I would love that, Harry. Thank you."

She climbed out of the carriage and he took her hand to help her out. "I'll see you in an hour." His smile was contagious and Eliza felt her mood lift as she walked into the bank.

Eliza found Minnie's office and, like before, her door was ajar slightly. Minnie had her hair piled in a bun and was staring intently at a newspaper and making notes in the margins. Eliza knocked lightly and Minnie looked up in surprise and delight. She jumped up and ran over to Eliza and pulled her for a hug.

"I am so glad to see you and I am so very sorry for your loss. Such a tragedy. I didn't realize he was sick." She had sent formal condolences as well. There was a huge stack of cards for all of them, and they were still arriving daily.

"No one did. It was sudden. It took us all by surprise."

"Have a seat. How are you doing?" Minnie looked at her closely and Eliza felt her eyes threaten to well up again. She took a deep breath and willed the tears back.

"It's been hard," she admitted. "I'm trying to keep busy today. To keep the sadness at bay."

Minnie nodded. "It's good to keep busy. We can talk about the market if you like? Your two stocks are up a bit."

That was exactly what Eliza needed. The time flew by as Minnie went over what she'd learned recently and shared her insights with Eliza. And she gave her update on her land sale.

"Richard from your uncle's office sent me a note to reassure me that our deal for the land is still on. We close in two weeks."

"Oh! That's good." Eliza hadn't given Minnie's land a thought since her father died. But she knew Richard was more than capable of running the business in her father's absence. She guessed that he would just report to her grandmother occasionally with updates. She was glad that the deal was still going through. It would be good for Minnie and it would have been good for her father, but now it would still be good for the company. So, that was something.

"Yes, and I have plans for that money." Minnie's eyes lit up.

"Oh? How will you invest it?" Eliza asked.

"Railroads." Minnie sat back and crossed her arms over her chest. "I've been steadily buying stock in several of them over the past few years and I study them quite closely. There are changes coming and I want to be there when they happen." She went on to explain some of her thoughts about where she thought things were headed. When they wrapped up their discussion, Minnie walked her out.

"I know I won't be seeing you at any of the upcoming events, though I try to avoid those as much as possible. Stop by any time if you want to say hello and have a chat. And keep the railroads we discussed in mind if you are ready to invest again."

"I will," Eliza promised her. She walked outside and Harry smiled and waved to her from the carriage, where he stood by the passenger door. He opened it as she approached, and she climbed in.

They drove off and rode past the familiar shops and department stores that Eliza was looking forward to visiting again. Harry pulled onto a side street a few blocks past the main shopping area. He stopped in front of a red brick building with a plain gray front door. As she got out of the carriage, Eliza noticed two men carrying huge boxes into the building across the street. Harry followed her gaze and smiled.

"They make wool coats and menswear. The owner was a good friend of my father's. I've known them for years. They'll be good neighbors. The whole street is in the retail manufacturing trade."

Harry unlocked the front door and stepped inside, motioning for Eliza to follow him. She stepped into a huge room with high ceilings, red brick everywhere, and windows along two sides—Harry had the corner of the building. It was a sunny day and light poured through the windows. Harry showed her around, pointing out the huge bolts of fabric and at least a dozen or so desks with sewing machines on them. Beyond that were large machines that he explained were looms.

"We'll be creating fabric, selling it and using it ourselves, so we'll have a bigger profit margin. And we can design the fabric exactly the way we want it and ensure the best quality by procuring the cotton and wool ourselves." Harry's enthusiasm was contagious.

"That's exciting. What will you make first?"

"To start, for men, we are going to focus on suits—pants and jackets. For women, cloaks and simple everyday dresses. We're starting with a small collection and will build from there."

"That sounds wonderful. Have you already hired people to help?"

Harry nodded. "My sisters and mother are starting right away with the sewing and a few cousins and some of their friends will be helping with the looms. I'll still need more help, though, once we get going."

Harry told her all about his plans and she was impressed that he already had tentative orders in place.

"I've talked to all the big department stores. Most of them knew my father and they want to see samples as soon as we can get them done. If they like what they see, they'll place a bigger order." Harry grinned. "And then we'll be off to the races!"

Eliza laughed. "I'm excited for you, Harry. I can't wait to see your clothing in the stores."

They strolled back to the main shopping district after leaving the factory and popped into a few shops, and then Harry led the way into the big department stores. As they walked through the men's and women's sections, Harry pointed out the new arrivals and paid close attention to what seemed to be of interest to shoppers.

"I like to stand back sometimes and just watch what people gravitate toward. At what they touch and ultimately what they decide to buy—as they are often very different things."

Eliza found it interesting too, and she couldn't help reaching out to touch the fabric of an elegant burgundy-colored dress. It felt luxurious and had a sheen to it. It wasn't very practical, though. It was more of a special occasion dress.

Harry smiled. "That is a lovely dress, but you're the third woman I've seen touch it and then move on to something else. We won't be producing many dresses like that. I want to create clothing that feels nice but that you also want to wear often."

The time flew by as they roamed the stores. Until a clock chimed that it was half-past two and Eliza's stomach rumbled. She hadn't given luncheon a thought, but now she was suddenly starving. She stopped at a street cart that sold hot roasted nuts. The smell was a tantalizing mix of sweet and savory as they were roasted with a bit of sugar until it caramelized. She bought two small bags, one for her and one for Harry. He didn't even realize it at first as he'd walked past and then turned back when he realized she wasn't beside him. He laughed when he saw her tear open a pack of nuts and happily accepted the bag she handed to him.

"Thank you. You didn't have to do that." He popped a cashew in his mouth and thought for a moment. "My mother's house is just a few blocks away. She'd love to meet you and today is pasta day. She makes a big pot of tomato sauce with meat and peppers. You've never had anything like my mother's sauce."

Eliza hesitated for a moment, taken by surprise by the invitation.

Harry grinned. "We really should eat more than a handful of nuts. My mother would be honored if you'd try her sauce. You can meet my sisters, too."

It did sound appealing. Eliza was curious about Harry's family and where he lived. "If you're sure they won't mind?"

He laughed at the thought of it. "It will make her day. I promise."

He led the way, and it was a short walk, just a few blocks to his family's home. They lived in a brownstone, a well-kept building on a tree-lined street.

Eliza followed him inside, to a kitchen where a woman in a simple gray dress and a white apron was stirring something in a big pot on the stove. She turned at the sound of footsteps and her face lit up with a big smile when she saw Harry. And her eyes were full of questions when she saw Eliza.

"What brings you round here in the middle of the day?"

Harry grinned. "I'm working. Meet Miss Eliza. Eliza, meet my mother."

"It's a pleasure to meet you, dear. I'm so very sorry about your uncle's passing."

"Thank you," Eliza said.

"Miss Eliza needed to do some shopping this way. I showed her the factory and told her she had to try your sauce. We haven't had luncheon yet."

"You must both be starving!" His mother quickly filled two plates with pasta and a generous helping of tomato sauce that was rich with onions and peppers and chunks of beef. Eliza's mouth watered as his mother set the food on the table and insisted that they sit and eat while it was hot.

"Will you join us?" Harry asked.

His mother shook her head. "I've had my fill. I was about to fix a cup of tea, though." She made the tea and joined them at the table.

Eliza had never had anything like Harry's mother's pasta before. It tasted as wonderfully as it smelled.

"You like it?" Harry asked after her first bite. "That sauce simmers for hours."

"It's so good."

His mother looked pleased with the compliment. "Thank you, dear. My mother was from Italy, Sicily and she taught me how to make the sauce. She called it gravy, and she would simmer it for hours with a big piece of meat for flavor. I make a batch of it every week, and it never lasts more than a few days."

She took a sip of her tea and studied both Eliza and Harry for a moment.

"Harry enjoyed working for your family. I know he'll miss you and the others."

"I will. Of course I will," Harry said.

"We'll all miss him." Eliza said softly and smiled. "I'm excited, though, for what Harry is building. He told me that you and his sisters will be helping."

His mother nodded. "We're all looking forward to it. The girls should actually be home any time now. They went to the store for me after luncheon to get some eggs and milk."

"Yesterday was everyone's last day at the factory," Harry said. He frowned. "They pay so poorly and expect the women to work sixteen-hour days. It's not right. And it won't be that way in my factory."

His mother glanced at him proudly. "I'll see to it that our quality is the absolute highest. Everyone will be well rested and grateful for the jobs."

"Sixteen-hour days? Is that what it's like at most of the factories?" Eliza couldn't imagine how horrible that must be.

Harry nodded. "They're all sweatshops. They take advantage of poor women, because they have no other options."

"That's so unfair," Eliza said.

"It's part of the reason why I'm determined to make this a success. It's not just for me—it's helping all the women in my family, and the other people we hire. It's my hope that other factories will follow my lead in time."

"Is Harry here?" Two women a bit younger than Eliza rushed into the kitchen. Both had dark hair like their brother, thick, long loose curls that they tamed into a bun of sorts—but a few wayward curls escaped and framed their faces. Both had big, brown eyes like their brother as well. One was a bit smaller and looked at Eliza with interest.

"Introduce us to your friend, Harry?"

"Of course. Eliza, meet my sisters—Penny and Constance."

"It's Connie now, Harry. Nice to meet you, Eliza." Connie was the small one and held her brother's gaze, waiting for more of an explanation.

"Eliza wanted to do some shopping and as we were in the area, we came by."

"You're the cousin, then? The new arrival at the Redfield home?" Connie asked.

"I'm so sorry about your uncle," Penny said softly.

"Yes, so sorry," Connie chimed in.

"It's lovely to meet you both," Eliza said. "I was hoping to get my mind off everything. It's been hard because I hadn't seen my….uncle in years and we were just growing close. I went to work with him every morning, so I've been feeling a bit adrift. And with today being Harry's last day, well, I think of him as good friend and it's someone else I'll be missing now."

"She wanted to go shopping, and I showed her the factory. I think she liked it," Harry said and grinned.

Eliza laughed. "It's really impressive and I understand you'll all be working there. It will be nice to build something together, I imagine?" After working briefly with her father, she couldn't help but think how lucky they all were.

Connie pulled out a chair and sat at the table, and Penny did the same. "We're excited. We both hated the factory."

Penny nodded. "It wasn't a good place to work."

They all chatted for another twenty minutes or so while Harry and Eliza finished eating. Eliza would have liked to stay longer. They were all so friendly and easy to talk to, and she felt more at home with them. She didn't have to worry about saying the wrong thing as she did at most of the events she went to where she had to have her wits about her. There was a warmth and sense of fun as the sisters teased their brother. It was clear they adored him, and his mother sipped her tea contentedly and chimed in now and then.

But Harry watched the clock and regretfully said he needed to be back to bring Alice for a final fitting at the dressmaker.

"It was so lovely to meet you all," Eliza said as they said their goodbyes.

"If you find yourself in the area on a weekend, please

stop in anytime to say hello," Harry's mother said after giving Eliza a warm hug.

"Your family is wonderful," Eliza said once they were on their way. She'd admired their closeness and affection they had for each other. It was very different from Eliza's frosty relationship with her sisters. She sighed. The days seemed to loom long and cold ahead of her. Her grandmother wasn't due home for several more weeks—her sister was still hanging in there, though they didn't expect she'd last much longer. There wouldn't be a funeral for her father until her grandmother returned to pick up his ashes from the crematorium.

"Thank you. I am lucky, and luckier still, that they all agreed to work with me. It will be the start of a new adventure." Eliza was thrilled for him, for all of them. She felt quite miserable for herself though—Harry was her first friend in the city and she hated the thought of not seeing him often.

When they reached the house, Harry held the door open for her and once she was out, she impulsively gave him a hug.

"I might not see you for a long time. I hope you are wildly successful, Harry. I know you will be." She smiled sadly, and he brushed her hair off her face.

"Truthfully, you are the only thing I'll miss about working here. If things were different..." He let the words trail off and Eliza's heart jumped.

"If they were?" She asked softly.

Harry shook his head. "Don't mind me. I'm just being

silly." He grinned. "I expect you'll be engaged, maybe even married, the next time we run into each other."

Eliza didn't think that was remotely likely, but she just nodded. Because Harry was right. It just wasn't done. Eliza knew that better than anyone.

"Goodbye, Harry."

25

The following week dragged on. Eliza tried to fill her time with long walks, and spent a great deal of time in the library, reading her way through the many leather-bound books. She enjoyed that, but she missed going into the office. It didn't feel right to go there until her grandmother returned, though. It was her father's business. What would she even do there without him?

She was used to sitting with her father, handling his correspondence, and talking to him about what he was working on. He told her in great detail of his plans for the new affordable housing development and he explained his decisions on various matters that needed his attention. She'd learned so much in a short amount of time about his approach to real estate development. She found she enjoyed it, but it wasn't the same now that he was gone.

Alice and Rose seemed to be doing fine. She hardly saw them, except at meals, where they still didn't bother with her much, and spoke mostly to each other. Eliza learned that they planned to spend most of the summer in Newport at the family cottage.

"The dreadful six months will be over by then and we can get back to normal. Nick and his family will be there for a few weeks before they go home to London," Alice said.

"Sissy Andrews saw him at a supper last night after the opera. She said he was flirting with all the girls, as usual, and that Millie Evans seems to have her eye on him. Do you know her? I'm not familiar with the name."

Alice narrowed her eyes. "I know who she is. She's barely eighteen, and this is her first season. She's a very pretty girl—blond with blue eyes." She smiled tightly, her thin lips just barely curving up, "But her family isn't nearly as rich as ours."

Late Friday afternoon found Eliza curled up on a window seat in the library, reading a book that Minnie had recommended, Charlotte Perkins Gilman's *The Yellow Wallpaper*. It was a fascinating story—a protest against women being thought inferior and controlled by their husbands. She was so deep into the story that at first she didn't hear Alice enter the room. But then she felt the shift in the air that always seemed to accompany Alice—a depressing coldness. Eliza looked up and Alice smiled slightly.

"Could you join Rose and I in the drawing room? Father's attorney is here for a reading of the will."

"Of course. I assumed that wouldn't happen until Grandmother returned."

"Mr. Davis thought we should discuss it before then," Alice said.

Eliza stood and walked with Alice to the drawing room where Rose was already seated in one of four chairs around a round table by the fireplace. It was a cold day, and the fire glowed merrily. An older man that Eliza assumed must be the attorney also sat at the table. They both stood when Eliza and Alice approached.

Alice introduced Eliza to the attorney, and they all sat around the table. Mr. Davis cleared his throat and reached for a sip of water before speaking. He opened a folder with a stack of papers in it.

"Your father's will is quite simple. He, uh…. he hasn't updated it in many years. So, his wishes haven't changed."

Eliza noticed that Rose and Alice exchanged glances. Rose looked a bit upset, while Alice looked positively smug. Eliza simply felt confused, and a sense of unease began to creep over her. Alice looked too happy.

"Your father has left everything in his estate to his two daughters equally." He paused before looking at Eliza. "Regretfully, it appears that he did not update his will to include anyone else."

Eliza was a bit surprised, but not upset. She'd never wanted anything from her father. She'd just been happy to find him and spend time with him. She'd hoped for a similar relationship with her sisters, but maybe there was still time for that.

But apparently, Alice didn't feel the same. "Rose and I have been talking and we think, now that father is gone, that it might be best for you to return to England. As there's really nothing here for you now."

Eliza was shocked. She glanced at Rose, but she was looking out the window, avoiding Eliza's gaze completely. "Is this really what you both want? You want me to leave?"

Alice nodded. "I think it would be best. Make a clean break."

Rose glanced at Eliza and looked miserable. "I'm so sorry." Eliza understood immediately what that meant. This was Alice's idea, and she'd forced Rose to go along with it.

"But, what about Miriam? She's with child. She can't lose her job now." Eliza was still trying to make sense of it all. Her sisters were actually asking her to leave, kicking her out of what had become her home.

"Oh, don't worry about Miriam," Alice said breezily. "My girl gave notice just this week, so she can take her place. It will work out perfectly."

"But, what about Grandmother? Surely, she should have a say in this? She will be back in another week or two."

Alice and Rose exchanged glances again, and Rose looked away.

"We wrote to Grandmother, and I heard back from her today, and she agrees that it's best if you go back to England. She never wanted you here, you know. It was all father's doing."

"She never wanted me here?" Eliza felt tears threaten to rise and spill over. She took a deep breath and willed them back. She refused to cry in front of Alice.

"I heard her and father fighting about it, more than once. She wasn't happy with the idea of you coming here at all. She thought it could be upsetting for everyone and she worried that word would get out about, well, you know."

Eliza lifted her chin and glared at Alice. "That didn't happen, though, did it?"

"Not yet. But we all want things to go back to the way they were."

Eliza stood. "Fine. I'll leave tomorrow then. Once I'm settled, I'll send for my things."

"This is for you," Mr. Davis said. He pulled an envelope out of the folder and handed it to Eliza.

"What is this?"

"It's a check. A small amount to cover your trip back to England and a bit more to tide you over until you are settled," he said.

"It's the least we could do," Alice said, as if they were being so very generous. Eliza was tempted to refuse the envelope but thought better of it and took it, for now. If she did go back to England, she would need the money to find a place to live. She had some cash in her room and the stocks and money in her bank account as well. Her mind was spinning as she tried to grasp that this was really happening.

"I'd like to have dinner in my room tonight." She couldn't fathom sitting at the dinner table with her sisters now.

Alice nodded. "Of course. And once you are settled, just send word and we'll have your trunks shipped for you." She smiled with satisfaction while Eliza's stomach suddenly clenched. She needed to get out of that room.

She stood. "Mr. Davis, it was nice meeting you." She glanced at Alice and then Rose, who finally met her eyes and looked close to tears.

"Goodbye Eliza," Rose said softly.

26

"Miriam, a word, please."

Miriam was on her way to Eliza's room to help her dress for dinner and turned at the sound of Alice's voice. She generally tried to avoid running into Alice. She'd had to fill in occasionally when one of Alice's maids had the day off and to say Alice was demanding was an understatement. Her turnover was so high—no one wanted to support her for long—they either quit or Alice fired them in one of her moods. Miriam knew that Lydia had quit a few days earlier, and she already felt sorry for whoever took the position next.

"Yes, of course." She followed Alice into the drawing room and waited. Alice didn't sit, so Miriam was grateful that this would be a brief conversation.

"I have some good news for you. As of tomorrow, you will be moving into a new role, as my ladies' maid."

Miriam's heart sunk. "But who will assist Miss Eliza?"

"Eliza is leaving us. She's going back to England tomorrow. Of course, we will miss her terribly."

Miriam looked closely at Alice. Her eyes didn't match her words. She looked positively gleeful at the news.

"That is sad news about Miss Eliza. She will be missed. I am, of course, grateful to assist you."

Alice nodded. "It is a wonderful opportunity for you. Eliza wishes to take her dinner in her room. Can you see to that, please?"

"Of course."

"That's all then. Thank you, Miriam." Alice swept out of the room, making a grand exit while Miriam stood still in utter shock and despair.

Eliza stopped packing when Miriam knocked softly at her bedroom door and entered a moment later carrying a dinner tray. She set it on the table by the window and removed the silver dome that covered the plate.

"Have they told you the news?" Eliza asked.

Miriam nodded and looked quite miserable. "Alice found me earlier and let me know that I'll be moving to assist her, and that you're going back to England tomorrow. I'm sorry to hear that. I thought you liked it here."

Eliza took a deep breath. "I do like it here. And I have a confession—I'm not going back to England."

The light came back into Miriam's face and Eliza realized she'd misunderstood.

"I'm not going back to England, but unfortunately, I can't stay here any longer."

"You can't? But why not? I don't understand."

"Now that my….uncle is gone, Alice let me know that the family thinks it's best for me to return to England. I don't think they were ever keen on me staying for long."

Miriam frowned. "I can believe it of Alice. But I wouldn't have thought Rose would feel the same. And I can't imagine your grandmother approves of this?"

"Alice said that she did. She wrote to her. It's disappointing, but I don't want to stay where I'm not wanted."

"Where will you go?"

"I told Alice and Rose that I would send for my things once I'm settled, and I may do that eventually." Eliza knew there was no hurry for that because where would she possibly wear those elegant gowns now? She'd still be in mourning for several more months and if everyone thought she was in England, there would be no invitations. Not that she minded about that. It was one thing she wouldn't miss—all those silly balls.

"I thought I might pay a visit to Harry and his family. They might know of a female boardinghouse that might be suitable." She told Miriam about her visit to Harry's mother's house. Miriam looked relieved.

"Good. They will know what to do and where you should go. But, what will you do for money? Do you have any savings with you?"

Eliza nodded. "I have some. Not much, but enough to get me settled somewhere. And I'll have to find work."

Miriam looked nervous at the thought of it. "What will you do for work?"

Eliza was tempted to tell her that they had more in

common that Miriam realized, but she thought it best to keep that to herself. "I can sew. I think there's always a need for that kind of work."

Miriam nodded. "There is. I considered it at one point, but my sewing skills are sorely lacking."

Eliza smiled. She didn't love sewing, but she was good at it and if she could use those skills to support herself, she would happily do so. She didn't dare take a job as a ladies' maid for fear that someone might recognize her. She still had her old dresses and if she mostly wore those and took a job in another part of the city in a factory, no one needed to know her whereabouts.

"Will you get in touch once you're settled? Just so I know that you're all right?"

"Of course." Eliza thought for a moment. She couldn't send a note directly to Miriam, or Alice and Rose might learn that she hadn't gone back to England after all. But Miriam was already one step ahead of her.

"Give a note to Harry to give to Colin. They see each other often and no one needs to be the wiser."

"Perfect."

"I'll see you in the morning, to help you dress and to say goodbye," Miriam said.

"Thank you, Miriam. Have a good night."

Miriam left the room and Eliza suddenly felt very alone as she ate her steamed codfish and gazed out the window. It was dark now and the street lamps glowed below as carriages drove by. She would miss this view.

anning, Mrs. Smith and Miriam all waited at the front door to bid Eliza farewell the next morning. Alice and Rose were nowhere in sight.

Eliza hugged them all goodbye and walked outside to where Colin was waiting to drive her to the ship. He took her bag, which was packed with all of her older dresses and several newer ones, just in case. She left everything else behind... all the beautiful ball gowns and the new black mourning dresses, aside from the one she was wearing. She hated them as they only served to remind her of her father's death, but practically, she didn't want to draw that kind of attention and questions either.

Colin helped her into the carriage and, a moment later, backed out of the driveway. He headed toward the ships, but as soon as they were out of sight from the house, he turned left onto a street and went in the opposite direction.

"Miriam told me about your plans. I'm driving you right to Harry's mother's house. They'll know what to do."

"Thank you, Colin."

Fifteen minutes later, they arrived. Eliza got out of the carriage, took the bag from Colin, and thanked him again.

"Anytime you want to reach Miriam, just give your note to Harry and he'll get it to me. Be well, Eliza."

Colin drove off and Eliza took a deep breath. She stepped up to the front door and knocked.

A moment later, the door swung open and Harry's mother looked surprised but happy to see her. She glanced at the large bag Eliza was holding, then silently pulled her in for a hug and squeezed her tight. Eliza relaxed, and the tears came gushing out of nowhere. She immediately reached for a handkerchief and dabbed at her eyes.

"Come in dear. I'll make you a cup of tea and you can tell me everything. Set your bag right down by the door. We'll worry about that later."

Eliza did as instructed and went into the kitchen with Harry's mother. She half-expected his sisters to be there, but the room was empty.

"Have a seat. Are you hungry? I just made a batch of corn muffins. They're Harry's favorite. Help yourself. Here's a plate and some butter." She set a knife and plate in front of Eliza and pushed the platter of muffins toward her. Eliza hadn't eaten since breakfast. She'd had no appetite for food that morning, but now suddenly she was starving. She reached for a muffin. It was still warm. She cut it in half, smeared a bit of soft butter across the top and took a bite and then another. She tasted warmth and love in every bite. And the thought made the tears threaten to erupt again. She took another bite and tried to just focus on how good the muffin was.

Harry's mother set a mug of tea on the table and a pot of sugar and sat across from Eliza and stirred a spoonful of sugar into her own mug.

"The girls are working today with Harry in the factory. They're young and have all the energy. I told Harry I'm too old to work weekends." She smiled and sipped her tea. "It's lovely to see you, my dear, but I don't think this is a happy visit. How can I help?"

The words came out in a rush as Eliza told her everything, including the fact that she'd worked as a ladies' maid in London.

"I should have known it would never last. I never quite felt like I belonged there."

Harry's mother listened quietly, and her eyes looked stormy when Eliza finished talking.

"Shame on them. The whole lot of them. You had every right to be there. Those girls are spoiled. I find it difficult to believe your grandmother feels the same way. Was she ever cold toward you, like Alice?"

"No. She never was. That's why it came as such a surprise."

"And all you have is Alice and Rose's word on this?"

"Yes, but their attorney was there, too. It all seemed very official."

Harry's mother took a sip of tea and looked deep in thought for a long moment.

"And they think you're on the ship back to England?"

Eliza nodded.

"Good, let them think that. You'll stay here tonight. You can have Connie's bed. She won't mind sleeping in Penny's room. They shared a room for years. When Harry moved into his own place, the girls got their own rooms."

"Oh, I don't want to do that. I can sleep on the sofa."

"Don't be silly. It's one night. You'll have dinner with us. Harry's coming and we'll all help you make a plan. This afternoon, we can visit Ida Bramhill, she has a female boardinghouse that might be appropriate for you. It's nearby and Ida is particular who she takes in. You'll be safe there and it won't be expensive. You do have some savings?"

Eliza nodded. "I do. Enough to get by, I think, until I can find a job of some sort."

"Can you sew?"

"Yes. I've never done it professionally, but I used to make all my own dresses."

"Good. Harry might be able to use you." She smiled proudly. "Macy's gave him an initial order that he needs to fill as soon as possible."

Eliza relaxed a bit. She was grateful to spend the night with Harry's family before moving into the boardinghouse. Even though she trusted it was a safe place, it was still a bit intimidating to be completely on her own.

After they finished their tea, they walked to the boardinghouse. It was just a few blocks away, maybe a ten-minute walk if that. It was a brownstone with a light pink door and a sign that read, Mrs. Bramhill's Boardinghouse —Females only.

They rang the bell and a short, thickset older woman with light gray hair worn in a tight bun opened the door and looked at them quizzically before she recognized Harry's mother.

"Mary, good to see you. What brings you here this fine morning?" Eliza detected a hint of an Irish accent.

"Ida, I'd like you to meet a friend of the family, Eliza Chapman." Harry's mother had suggested that Eliza only use her mother's surname and avoid any mention of the Redfield connection.

"It's lovely to meet you," Eliza said politely.

"If you have room, Eliza is in need of a place to stay for a while."

Mrs. Bramhill addressed Eliza. "I might have a room. How long were you planning to stay?"

Eliza hesitated. "I'm really not sure. Several months, at least I suppose, quite possibly longer."

Mrs. Bramhill nodded. Eliza supposed it was normal for boardinghouse guests to stay for varying lengths of time.

"You can stay for a week at a time. Every Sunday, you'll pay for the following week. Would you like to come in and see the room?"

"Yes, please." They followed Mrs. Bramhill inside, through a spacious study where there was a cheerful fireplace. Two young women sat nearby, chatting and working on needlepoint and knitting. They went up to the second floor and down a long hallway before Mrs. Bramhill unlocked a door and they all stepped inside.

It was a small room, with just a bed, dresser, tiny table and chair in the corner. But the ceiling was high, at least ten feet or so, which made it seem more spacious, and there was a large window with a view of the street. Eliza immediately felt comfortable and could see herself staying there. It would do just fine. Provided she could afford it.

"It's lovely. May I ask what your rent is for the room?"

Mrs. Bramhill told her and the amount was reasonable. Eliza could afford it, but she would have to watch her spending, as she had to stretch her savings for as long as possible. Hopefully, Harry could give her some work, but if not, she would have to find something else.

Harry's mother looked around the room and walked closer to the window to take a better look at the view. "What do you think?" She asked Eliza.

"I'd like to take it. How soon could I move in?"

"As soon as tomorrow." They went downstairs to Mrs. Bramhill's office and Eliza paid her for the first week's rent and received a key to the room.

"Well, that's settled," Harry's mother said as they walked home. "Now we can go to the market and pick up some groceries for supper and you can help me make the ravioli. Have you done that before?"

"No, never. But I'd love to learn."

Eliza spent the rest of the afternoon helping Harry's

mother shop at the local market. They carried home bags of fresh vegetables, meat, cheese, flour and eggs. Eliza learned how to make ravioli pasta dough from flour, eggs and water and to roll it into long sheets across the kitchen table. They let the dough rest a bit while they made the filling—a mix of sausage, three cheeses and spinach.

Harry's mother showed Eliza how she made her Sunday gravy, too—the simple tomato sauce that she made each week. She minced a bit of onion and garlic, stirred it into a few swirls of olive oil and once it softened, added a hunk of meat, browned it on all sides before adding the crushed tomatoes. She let the sauce simmer for several hours while they finished filling and cooking the ravioli.

When everything was ready, Harry's mother layered ravioli and sauce on a large serving platter. She added the final batch of ravioli, more sauce, and a generous sprinkling of parmesan cheese as the front door opened and a chorus of voices poured into the room. Harry and his sisters laughed and talked loudly as they walked into the kitchen. They all stopped short when they saw Eliza.

"We have some unexpected company for dinner," Harry's mother said brightly. "Eliza helped me to make the ravioli and she'll be staying here tonight. Connie, you'll sleep in Penny's room."

Connie just nodded, while Harry's eyes were full of questions.

"Fill your plates and Eliza will explain over dinner. Penny, pour us all a glass of chianti."

They all settled around the table with their pasta and

wine. Eliza took her first bite of the ravioli and closed her eyes for a moment to better savor the flavors. She'd never tasted anything like it before. The pasta was soft and silky and the filling was cheesy and savory. The sauce was fragrant with meat and tomato, and the dusting of parmesan brought it all together. They ate hungrily and went back for seconds. As they ate, Eliza filled them all in on what had transpired. Connie and Penny were equally horrified on her behalf and Harry just looked angry.

"I'm disappointed in those girls, Alice, especially but also Rose, for letting her sister talk her into going along with this. I'm willing to bet your grandmother has no idea —and that Alice never wrote to her at all."

The thought had crossed Eliza's mind as well. "You really think she'd be that brazen?"

Harry laughed. "Alice has little regard for anyone other than herself. She has her sights set on that Nick Archibald and I suspect she sees you as a threat and simply wanted you out of the way."

"That is positively diabolical!" Penny said.

"Is she really capable of that, do you think?" Connie asked.

"I don't know. It's hard to imagine," Eliza said. "The lawyer showed me the will. It does make sense that my father hadn't gotten around to updating it yet. I hadn't been with them for very long. And unfortunately, it is also believable that my grandmother might not have been keen about me coming to New York. It would be embarrassing to the family if my true identity were to become known. It could hurt Alice and Rose's place in society to have an illegitimate sister."

"It's just not right," Harry insisted. "When your grandmother returns, you should go see her and ask her for yourself. See where the truth lies."

The thought of doing that and having her grandmother confirm that she did in fact prefer that Eliza return to England was a depressing thought and a conversation Eliza wasn't sure she wanted to have.

"I'll think about that. Right now, I just want to carve out a new place for myself—without the Redfield name."

"Eliza has sewing skills," his mother commented.

Harry smiled. "Good, you'll come work with us, then. We could use the help and you'll enjoy it. The work isn't the most exciting, but we try to have fun. And it's busy—we just landed a big order with Macy's." His eyes lit up, and he sat taller in his chair.

"I heard. That's such good news. I'm so happy for you, Harry." Eliza looked around the table. "I can't thank you all enough."

"It's nothing. You're a friend of the family," his mother said.

"And we take care of our friends," Harry said.

After dinner, Eliza helped wash the dishes and then went for a walk with Harry.

"I always like to move around a bit after one of my mother's pasta dinners," he said as they stepped outside. It was a cool evening and there were quite a few people out walking.

Eliza laughed. She'd eaten more than she normally would. The ravioli were so good and she was making up for hardly eating a thing for the past few days. She always lost her appetite completely when she was upset. After a very stressful day and night, she was feeling much calmer and hopeful about her future. She might not live in the Redfield mansion any longer, but she had a place to stay now, good friends and a new job.

She had enough savings with her that she could also hold off going to the bank to sell her stocks and withdraw what was left of her savings. She'd worried about that and about being recognized. But if the job worked out, she might be able to live on what she earned.

"This is a big change for you. I'm sorry that your sisters behaved so badly." Harry said as they walked along.

"I told your mother earlier. I never truly felt like I belonged there. I'm not sure where I belong. But before I came here, I worked all my life in service. It felt strange to have my own ladies' maid," she admitted.

"What will happen to Miriam now?" Harry frowned, worrying about his friends.

"She has been promoted. She'll be supporting Alice. She had another maid quit."

"They never last long with her, do they? Poor Miriam. But at least it's a job and they have housing."

"Miriam's wonderful. I can't imagine Alice will be able to find any fault with her work."

"Let's hope not." They walked along in comfortable silence until Harry glanced her way. "I never would have guessed that you were once a ladies' maid. You looked as though you belonged in that house. You did belong."

Eliza smiled. "Thank you. I'll be fine though. Thank you for the job. I won't let you down." She was grateful that she wouldn't have to search for a job and she'd heard rumors of the conditions in other factories.

"I know you won't." He smiled and held her gaze a moment longer than normal. Things suddenly felt different with Harry. He took her arm and pulled her closer to him as a carriage sped by and splashed water onto the sidewalk. It had rained during the night and there were puddles on the pavement. Harry's touch gave Eliza a sense of something new and exciting. He met her gaze again and smiled, and she felt warm inside. These were new feelings, like nothing she'd experienced before with any other man. For the first time, Eliza felt a sense of hope and of new possibilities.

As they walked, Harry told her all about the company and how things were going. His enthusiasm was contagious.

"We have the Macy's order and I think the other shops will be watching to see how well we sell. And then I have every confidence they will all jump on board and place their own orders."

They discussed what the order consisted of and what Harry would have her work on first. "I'll put you on the women's cloaks. Connie can show you the ropes and my mother can help answer any questions you might have, as well."

"Where do you live, Harry?" Eliza thought back to his mother's comment earlier that Connie had taken over his room when he moved out.

He grinned. "I live with two other fellows. We have an apartment just a few blocks from here, near the factory."

"That's convenient."

"It is. And the girls were tired of sharing a room."

They were almost back to the house and when they reached the front door, Harry asked, "Are you ready for dessert? My mother made an apple pie this morning and I'm almost ready for a slice."

"I couldn't, possibly." Eliza was still full from dinner. But when they went back inside, there were plates of pie on the table for all of them and she somehow found room. Connie played the piano after they finished dessert and they spent the rest of the evening laughing and occasionally singing along to the music. When Eliza went to bed, she fell asleep almost as soon as her head hit the pillow and slept soundly.

2 8

The next day was Sunday and Eliza went to church with Harry's family and his mother insisted that she join them for the mid-day meal, which was leftover ravioli. She also sent Eliza home with a basket of corn muffins, an apple, and some bread and cheese for her supper. Eliza accepted it gratefully and set out that afternoon to settle in at the boardinghouse. She had two books with her and read for a bit in her room, taking breaks every so often to gaze out the window and take in the view of the people and carriages on the street below. There was a sense of energy and possibility in the air, and Eliza felt hopeful that she could find her way.

She went to bed early and woke earlier than usual. She wanted to make sure she arrived at the factory on time for her first day. She washed up, changed into one of her older dresses and nibbled on a corn muffin before heading off to work.

Harry was there when she arrived and he showed her to the desk where she would be working. The others arrived soon after, and Connie and Penny sat at the desks beside her. Harry's mother handed her a pile of heavy wool fabric and explained that she'd be cutting it according to the pattern guide. She then showed her where she'd be stitching. They each had different pieces of the women's cloaks to work on. Once all the parts were sewn, they'd be stitched together and buttons sewn on.

It took Eliza a little time to get the hang of it, as she hadn't done any sewing in a while. But it came back to her quickly and soon she found herself in a rhythm of cutting and sewing. They took a short break at noon and Eliza ate the apple she'd brought with her. On her way home, she would buy some bread and meat for sandwiches. Mrs. Bramhill had shown her the icebox in the common area where guests could keep some food cold.

"Eliza, I packed something for you." Harry's mother surprised her with a ham and cheese sandwich, which Eliza happily accepted.

"Thank you so much. I'll bring my own tomorrow."

Eliza fell into a routine over the next few weeks. The factory was busy, and the days flew by. They were long shifts though, they were all working nine and ten-hour days to meet the deadline for the Macy's order. By the time Eliza returned to her small room at the boardinghouse, she was tired and most nights she could only manage to eat a light supper of cheese and bread before curling up with a cup of hot tea and a newspaper or novel for a few hours before going to bed and doing it all again the next day. On Sundays, she joined Harry's family at church and spent the afternoon at their home enjoying Sunday dinner and a walk after, with Harry.

Eliza looked forward to Sundays. She enjoyed the warmth and friendship of his family, but it was the walks with Harry that she most looked forward to. She grew to admire him the more she spent time with him. Harry was handsome but also driven yet thoughtful, and he made her laugh. And she loved hearing him talk about his dreams. They were so real to him that she didn't doubt that his plans for a department store of his own would one day come to pass, and that it would be a success.

Eliza sensed mutual interest from Harry to deepen their friendship, and she waited for him to officially ask to court her, but he didn't seem to be in any hurry to do so. She wondered if it might be because she was working for him, or if he worried she might return to her grandmother's world. Eliza didn't think that was likely. And even if she did take her place in society again, she still wanted to pursue a relationship with Harry.

He was the only man she was interested in and she knew he didn't think it was a good idea to mix those worlds, but she disagreed. If not now, then when? Eliza felt that things needed to change, and that Mrs. Astor and her antiquated notion of only four hundred people deemed 'acceptable' was quite ridiculous.

She was also curious how Minnie was doing and longed

to visit her at the bank and chat about the market. As much as she enjoyed working at the factory with Harry and his family, the work wasn't intellectually stimulating and she missed being involved with her father's business. She read the business papers and followed the markets as best as she could and was intrigued to see recent mentions of volatility with the railroad stocks. Minnie was definitely onto something there. Though she didn't dare visit her and risk someone recognizing her and word getting back to her family. Not yet.

A little over a month after Eliza left, a note came through Harry, from Miriam. Eliza had just arrived at the factory and, as usual, was the first in, though the others would be along any moment. She carefully opened the note, which had been sealed with a pretty blue wax stamp.

Eliza, hope you are well. Wanted to inform you that your grandmother is due to arrive home tomorrow and a funeral service is scheduled for the following day at their home. I don't think your grandmother knows you are not here. You should go. Service is at eleven.

She was shocked. She'd assumed that her grandmother had returned several weeks ago and that the funeral had already happened. She'd watched the papers for notice of it, but hadn't seen anything and assumed it may have been a private service. This was the most unexpected news. And there was no time to arrange a visit with her grandmother first. If she decided to attend the service, she would simply arrive along with everyone else. She could only imagine the looks on Alice and Rose's faces when she walked in.

29

"Grandmother is more upset than I imagined she would be about Eliza leaving," Rose said nervously. She was sitting on a chair in Alice's bedroom, while Miriam arranged Alice's hair. It was Saturday morning and Rose was already dressed and ready for the funeral.

As usual, Miriam was invisible to Alice. She didn't hesitate to speak her mind in front of her. Miriam supposed it would never cross her mind that Miriam would keep in touch with Eliza. Especially as Alice thought that Eliza had returned to England. Miriam smiled as she imagined the look of shock upon Alice's face when Eliza walked into the church. If she attended. Miriam fervently hoped that she would.

"She did seem a bit confused by it all. I thought she would have been used to the idea by now. I wrote her with the news as soon as Eliza left," Alice said.

"She just doesn't understand why Eliza would leave. She thought she liked it here. And that she would at least wait until she returned, to say a proper goodbye."

"That was rather inconsiderate of Eliza, wasn't it?" Alice chuckled and glanced at Rose, but her sister just shook her head and stared out the window.

"This is for the best, Rose. Remember that, please." Alice returned her gaze to the mirror and turned her head to admire Miriam's handiwork. She had carefully swirled Alice's hair into an elegant French twist.

Rose said nothing and continued staring out the window.

"You have to admit, it's much nicer without Eliza here. Everything is back to normal now. Better than normal, now that Nick has finally proposed." Alice held her hand up, and the ring was truly stunning. Miriam remembered Alice boasting about how it was Nick's grandmother's ring. It had a delicate setting with an abundance of rose-cut diamonds and it glittered in the sunlight as Alice admired it. "I couldn't be sure of that happening with Eliza around," Alice added.

Rose shot an angry glare at her sister. "Nothing is normal. Father is dead, in case you have forgotten. And Eliza never did a thing to you. She never seemed remotely interested in Nick, other than as a friend. I regret that she left the way that she did."

Alice narrowed her eyes at her sister. "Be careful, Rose. It's important that we keep our stories straight. We don't want to confuse Grandmother any further. She is getting up there in age, you know."

"Really, Alice. Grandmother is as sharp as a tack and you know it."

Alice sniffed. "I thought she seemed a bit forgetful at dinner last night."

"She was likely just exhausted. She is almost seventy-five, after all. And it had been a long day of traveling. A long week, actually."

"Right. Well, anyway, Eliza's gone and there's not a thing we can do about it. We all have to move on."

Rose sighed. "Yes, I suppose we do."

Alice stood. "That's all, Miriam. Thank you. Rose, let's go downstairs and get this over with."

"Would you like me to go in with you?" Harry asked.

He'd driven Eliza to her grandmother's house for the funeral service. She'd barely managed to get a cup of tea down that morning while she dressed. She couldn't eat a thing. As much as she wanted Harry's support, she knew that she needed to face her grandmother and her sisters alone. They'd arrived fifteen minutes early.

"I'd love that, but I think I need to do this myself."

Harry nodded. "Very good. I'll wait here until others go in and then pay my regards."

Eliza took a deep breath before stepping out of the carriage.

"Good luck, Eliza."

She nodded her thanks and slowly made her way to the front door and stepped inside.

Canning was the first to see her, and his initial shock was quickly replaced with delight.

"Miss Eliza, it's so good to see you. Go right into the front parlor. Your grandmother and cousins are there. No one else has arrived yet."

"Thank you, Canning. It's good to see you too." Eliza walked toward the front parlor and slowed her steps when she saw her sisters standing by her grandmother. Her grandmother looked older than when she'd last seen her. Her eyes held the pain of losing her sister and her son. They all looked up when Eliza entered the room. Her grandmother's face lit up, and she took a step toward her.

"Eliza! I thought you left us. I'm so happy to see you here." She pulled Eliza in for a hug.

Rose's expression was a mix of nervousness and confusion while the look on Alice's face could only be described as pure, unadulterated fury.

"What are you doing here? You said you were going back to England?" Alice hissed.

"Actually, that's what you told me to do. I decided to stay." Eliza couldn't help but notice Alice's engagement ring and assumed it was from Nick. She'd finally gotten everything she'd wanted, Eliza out of the picture and an engagement to Nick.

"Where have you been, my dear? I've been so worried." Her grandmother was still holding onto her hand and gave it a squeeze.

Eliza was about to tell her everything, but as she opened her mouth to speak, several people walked into the room to pay their regards.

"I'll tell you everything, once everyone leaves Grandmother."

Her grandmother nodded as one of her dearest friends smiled and headed their way. "All right, dear. I agree, it's best to wait."

Harry came in a few minutes later and was polite to Alice and Rose and sincerely expressed his condolences to her grandmother. He whispered in Eliza's ear—"Shall I wait to give you a ride home?"

Eliza shook her head. "No, I am going to be here for a while. We're going to talk after everyone leaves."

"Very well. Best of luck, Eliza."

Two hours later, after the final guest left and only family remained, Eliza's grandmother motioned for them all to have a seat.

"Now, Eliza, please explain to me what has transpired in my absence and why I was told you no longer wished to live here and had returned to England?"

"Alice and Rose had me meet with father's attorney for a reading of the will. I was told that I wasn't welcome here, and that it was everyone's wish for me to return to England."

Eliza's grandmother folded her hands in her lap and

glanced at Alice and Rose, the latter of whom was fidgeting in her seat, while her sister defiantly returned their grandmother's gaze.

"You met with Mr. Davis? That's odd. I was under the impression that he was abroad for several months. He informed you then about your father's wishes?"

And now it was Eliza's turn to be confused. "Yes, I think so. I was told that everything was left equally to Alice and Rose."

Eliza's grandmother looked directly at Alice. "That's not quite true, is it?"

Rose spoke up, "I saw the will myself. That is what it says."

"Father updated the will," Alice said. "But he left a copy of the old one as well."

"And that's what you showed your sisters?"

Alice nodded.

"Mr. Davis wasn't here, was he? Who was it that met with the three of you and passed himself off as an attorney?"

Eliza leaned forward, curious to learn who it was.

"That was John Hendrix."

Her grandmother gasped. "The gardener I fired for drinking on the job?"

"Yes. He was eager for work and I paid him cash."

"Alice, I'm so disappointed in you. Tell your sister what your father's will actually says."

"You can tell her," Alice said sullenly.

Eliza's grandmother stood and left the room, returning

a moment later holding the updated will, which she handed to Eliza. "Your father updated this the day after you arrived. The three of you are to split his estate equally. And just a week before his death, he added an amendment. I'm not sure if Alice saw this, so perhaps you'd like to read it aloud?" Her grandmother pointed to the additional page and amendment in question.

"Eliza has taken a genuine interest in my business and has shown a keen aptitude for real estate development. It is my wish that she may choose to involve herself in the running of the business as much or as little as she desires. While Richard Owens will continue to manage the operations of the business, Eliza will have the final say on how things are run and can make any changes as she sees fit. For her role in the business, she will also draw a salary and a percentage of the company profits. All profits beyond that amount will be equally split between Eliza, Alice and Rose."

Alice's jaw dropped. Rose looked equally stunned, but not as horrified as her sister. "Eliza gets an additional share of the business? So, she's actually getting more than us? That doesn't seem at all fair," Alice complained.

"I think it seems very fair. She will simply be compensated—well compensated for any work that she does. Which will also benefit the two of you." She glanced at Rose. "Do you have a problem with this, too?"

Rose shook her head. "No, of course not. Not at all." She glanced at Eliza. "I'm so very sorry for my role in this. Can you ever forgive me?"

PAMELA KELLEY

Eliza nodded. "Yes." She knew that none of this had been Rose's idea.

"Alice, what were you thinking? You owe your sister an apology as well," their grandmother said sharply.

Alice was quiet for a long moment before finally muttering, "I am sorry. Perhaps I went a bit too far. I just wanted things to go back to the way they were."

Eliza's grandmother shook her head. "That ship sailed a long time ago. I'm quite horrified at your behavior, Alice. Your father's wish was for you and Rose to welcome Eliza. She's your sister."

Alice said nothing. Rose's eyes were red, and she dabbed at them with her handkerchief. She quite clearly felt awful, and Eliza guessed she'd been conflicted the entire time. Eliza wondered if Alice had ever shed a tear for anyone other than herself.

"Perhaps it might be best if you took dinner in your room, Alice, and have a long think about your actions. I will not tolerate any further behavior or disrespect from you. And I will also think about something else for you to do to make amends. Lastly, Miriam will return to assisting Eliza. The two of you can share a maid until you find a replacement. You are both excused. I'd like to speak to Eliza alone."

Alice and Rose left the room and once they were gone, Eliza's grandmother spoke.

"I cannot apologize enough for my granddaughters' shameful behavior. I'm disappointed that Rose couldn't put a stop to her sister's deception and chose to go along with

228

it. I want you to know that, like your father, I want you here very much. I certainly never wanted you to leave. When Alice informed me that you were going to return to England, I felt sick to my stomach."

"I'm so glad to know that you didn't feel that way. Alice was quite convincing, and it was heartbreaking. I truly don't care about the will. I was just grateful to get to know my family."

Her grandmother frowned. "Where have you been staying, my dear? You must come home at once."

Eliza smiled. It was nice to feel included, to think of her father's home as hers as well. Part of her was tempted to stay at the boardinghouse and continue working at the factory, but she knew that wasn't the right thing to do. Her grandmother was her only family, and she wanted Eliza to move home. So she would. She explained about the female boardinghouse and the work she'd been doing at the factory with Harry and his family.

"I'm grateful that they have been watching over you. Harry is a fine young man. And his new company already is working with Macy's? That is impressive. Do you think that you will wish to return to your father's office? You don't have to work at all, you know. Most women don't. And Richard will do a fine job managing the business. He has worked with your father for many years."

Eliza smiled. "I can't wait to go back to the office. I've really missed it. I've been grateful for the work with Harry's company, but I miss the challenge of the real estate business."

Her grandmother nodded. "Your father was very proud of you, you know. He said you showed a real aptitude for it. I always found it interesting as well. Your father often discussed his projects with me. While I don't have his direct experience, I do offer a certain perspective and sometimes it helps to discuss an idea with someone—to think it through out loud. I'm happy to help in that same way with you, as needed."

"I would love that. I value your opinion and your experience." Eliza was quiet for a moment. "I do worry a bit about Alice, though. She quite clearly doesn't want me here."

Her grandmother gave Eliza's hand a squeeze. "Don't you worry about Alice. I promise you she won't cause any further trouble. Not if she knows what is good for her."

30

*E*liza went to church the next morning as usual for the Sunday service. And over the mid-day dinner at Harry's mother's house, she filled everyone in on the dramatic events of the day before.

Harry didn't look surprised by any of it.

"I knew Alice was up to no good. I'm so glad you got everything sorted."

"And you're actually in the will." Penny sounded impressed.

It still hadn't really sunk in yet, though, that Eliza was now one of the wealthiest women in the city. Her father's estate was vast, with many real estate holdings, investments, and income from the business.

"I'm just thrilled for you, Eliza. Though we will miss you at the factory," Harry's mother said.

"I know this is short notice. It's all so sudden. I could

work out the week. I don't want to slow anything down for you."

But Harry shook his head. "We'll miss you, like my mother said. But I hired two more people and they both start this week. They're experienced and just left another factory. We'll be fine."

As usual, after dinner, Eliza and Harry went for a walk. She noticed that Harry seemed a bit distant and distracted. But she supposed it was just the suddenness of it all. As excited as she was to go back to the real estate work and move back into the mansion with her grandmother and sisters, she couldn't help but worry that this might mean a change in her relationship with Harry. But part of her wondered if it could be a good thing. Maybe now that she wouldn't be working for him, he might be more comfortable courting her. She hoped so.

"I'll miss working with you all every day," she said. She wanted to say she'd miss him, but she didn't want to be too forward.

Harry smiled. "It won't be the same without you there. I hope you won't forget about us all."

"Of course not! I'll see you next Sunday at church and maybe for dinner after, if your mother invites me," she teased.

"You're always welcome. I hope you know that." He held her gaze for a moment, and she felt his warmth and caring. "Can I give you a lift home? No sense carrying your bag the whole way." Eliza had packed everything she brought with her into her one bag before she headed to church. She'd planned to return to the boardinghouse to collect it and make the long walk home.

"If it's not too much trouble, I would appreciate that."

"Let's go."

She walked back to the house with Harry and he drove her to the boardinghouse and then home. It felt a bit strange to pull into the driveway with Harry driving.

"This is so familiar, and yet so much has changed."

Harry jumped out and opened the door for her, just like he used to do.

"Everything has changed," he agreed. "But change is good. Though it can also be hard at times." He looked as though he was remembering how things used to be as well, and where they were going now.

"Thank you, Harry. For everything. I really am going to miss you," she admitted.

He smiled. "I'm not going anywhere. I'll see you soon." He gave her a quick hug and then he was on his way. She watched him drive off, then picked up her bag and walked toward the front door. For the first time, she felt like she was actually home.

---

*I*t was good to be home. Eliza enjoyed a quiet dinner with her grandmother that evening. Rose had opted to have dinner in her room as well. Eliza guessed that she was mortified over her role in the deception and wasn't up to attending dinner without Alice by her side. It was nice to have her grandmother all to herself. It was the first time they'd had a lengthy, in-depth conversation and her grandmother told her all about her sister in England and how she'd managed to live longer than they'd expected. Once her grandmother arrived, her sister had rallied, and they'd had several weeks together to share so many memories and reminisce. Eliza knew her grandmother had prepared herself for her sister's death, but she'd been blindsided by the news of Eliza's father's sudden death.

"He was a special man, your father. He was smart and kind. His only fault was that he spoiled your sisters and their mother only made things worse. She was used to getting everything that she wanted and seems to have passed that trait on to Alice. Rose isn't quite so bad. I just wish she could stand up for herself more, instead of walking in Alice's shadow."

"Rose seems like a kind person. I hope to get to know her better." Eliza didn't add that she'd given up on getting to know Alice better. She wanted as little to do with her as possible.

"Once Alice marries, I think Rose will come into her own. I did notice there seemed to be a young man, Paul Dorfman, that has taken interest."

Eliza tried to place the name. She'd met so many people at the various balls and parties. Now that her grandmother mentioned it, though, she had noticed a tall, very thin man with black hair dancing with Rose more than once. She described him to her grandmother, and she nodded.

"That's him. He's a respectable fellow, from a good family. I believe he is a junior attorney with his father's firm. A bit on the shy, quiet side."

Eliza smiled. "He sounds perfect for her."

"He does, doesn't he? Though now that we're all in mourning, that is a bit of a challenge, though. That will be up by the summer though, and then we'll be off to Newport. I believe his family has a cottage there as well, so he and his father will be there on weekends."

Later that evening, as Miriam helped Eliza to get ready for bed, Eliza asked how she was feeling.

"It's still hard to tell in these dresses, but my stomach has grown quite a lot in these past few weeks. And I'm feeling well. Much better now that you're back." Miriam grinned.

"Was she just awful?" Eliza asked.

Miriam was silent for a moment before laughing. "What do you think? Alice can't help but be Alice."

"I can't thank you enough for getting that note to me."

"Of course. I knew something wasn't right. You belong here."

"It is good to be back." When Miriam left, Eliza crawled into bed and pulled the soft, plush covers over her. For the first time since arriving in America, she relaxed fully—and released the tension she didn't realize she'd been holding for so long. She let herself go and drifted off to sleep, feeling safe and secure that this time, she was home for good.

31

*E*liza woke feeling deeply refreshed and eager to start the day. She took breakfast early and read the paper while she sipped her coffee and ate her eggs and toast. Everyone was still sleeping, and the house was calm and quiet when she set off for the office. Colin drove her, and she thanked him for getting Miriam's note to Harry.

"Of course. It was my pleasure. Miriam and I were both eager to see that situation sorted. We're glad you're back. I know Miriam is happy to return to assisting you."

Colin dropped Eliza at the front door and asked if she'd like him to return at noon. She'd always done half days before.

"I think I'll spend a full day here. If you could return at five, that would be lovely."

Colin looked surprised, but quickly nodded before going on his way.

Eliza stepped inside. She was the first to arrive. Before

walking down the long hallway to her father's office, she collected the mail, which was in an overflowing box just inside the front door. She set it on her father's desk and took a moment to look around the room—at the tall grandfather clock in the corner, the small desk she'd been using and her father's sturdy oak desk, which overlooked the street. She glanced out the window, admiring the view. There was a lot of traffic, people walking and carriages going by as people headed into work. Eliza went to the small kitchen area and poured herself a glass of water before settling at her father's desk. His chair was upholstered in a soft leather and she thought she was likely imagining it, but she almost thought she could sense his presence in the room.

"I'll do my best to make you proud," she whispered as she sorted the mail into piles of bills, invitations, and miscellaneous. There weren't many bills, and they were all very recent. She guessed that Richard likely kept an eye on the mail and dealt with anything that looked urgent. She paid all the bills first, and was reading the first invitation when the front door opened and she heard voices. Several of the men that worked for her father arrived at the same time and headed to their offices. None of them even noticed that she was there. They would have to walk all the way to the end of the hall and look inside the office to see her behind her father's desk. She wondered how long it would take before someone realized she was there.

It didn't take long. Ten minutes later, Richard stepped

into the office and frowned when he saw Eliza seated at her father's desk.

"I noticed that the mail wasn't where I left it. I am surprised to see you here. Are you just stopping by?" He seemed both confused and less than pleased to see her.

Eliza smiled. Richard had always been a bit prickly towards her. She'd seen all the men in the office at her father's funeral, but their conversation had been brief. And at the time, Eliza had no idea about the amendment to her father's will. Since she was going to be spending more time in the office, she hoped that Richard might thaw out a bit.

"I'm actually going to be working here now. My uncle wanted me to step into his shoes. Not that I could ever fill his shoes, of course, but I intend to try. To do my best."

Richard looked dubious. "You plan to work here? Full-time? What will you do?"

Eliza cleared her throat and tried not to feel intimidated. Richard was a big man, with a big personality. "Well, I'm still learning, of course. So, I thought I would just sit in on meetings and help out where I can."

He raised his eyebrows. "You want to help out? The floor in my office needs sweeping." His tone was so disdainful that it took her by surprise.

She took a deep breath and tried not to show her anger. "That wasn't quite what I had in mind. I actually brought this with me, in case you needed clarification for what my uncle had in mind." Eliza handed him the amendment to the will, which spelled out that her father had complete confidence in Eliza, and that she had the final say and free rein to do as she wished. She watched as he read it and noticed a muscle in his jaw clench. He handed the paper back to her.

"I'll be in my office."

Eliza spent the rest of the day studying files from her father's recent projects and some older ones, too. She read through all of his notes as the projects progressed and took some of her own notes to understand the planning process and budget timelines. There were years of files to review and she intended to spend most of her time that week learning as much as she could about what her father had done and why he made the choices that he did on each project.

She noticed that Richard held several closed-door meetings in the conference room that she was not invited to. She allowed it as it was her first day in her new role and she didn't want the other men to think she was being difficult. She knew she needed them all to keep her father's business running.

But after today, she planned to attend any future meetings....whether she was invited or not.

32

*I*n some ways, it was as if Eliza had never left. Alice and Rose resumed attending the evening dinners with their grandmother, and Alice still barely spoke to Eliza. Rose did try to make more of an effort. Eliza could tell that she regretted going along with her sister's scheme. Alice's only regret was that she got caught.

Though they were still in mourning and not going to any evening social events, her sisters and grandmother attended several daytime luncheons and resumed meeting with the various charities they supported. They were all involved with the local suffragette efforts and after hearing her grandmother discuss it, Eliza was interested in learning more.

"You should come with us to our next meeting, Eliza. It will be worth missing a morning in the office," her grandmother said.

Alice made a face. "How can you stand being in that office all day? Don't you get bored?"

"I really don't. I still have so much to learn. I find it all fascinating." Eliza had managed to sit in on several planning meetings for ongoing projects and mostly listened as the men gave status updates. Richard still wasn't all that friendly, but he at least seemed to be tolerating her presence, so that was something.

"I always found it interesting too," her grandmother said.

"Yes, but you never went into the office. No one does that," Alice said.

"I didn't have to go anywhere. Your grandfather and then your father filled me in every evening. We had some lively discussions. They valued my opinion."

"She'll never find a husband that way." Alice didn't look entirely disappointed at the thought.

"I don't think that has to be true," Rose said. "Some men might quite like the idea of talking business with Eliza."

Alice looked dubious. "Talking business, perhaps. But would they want to marry her? To have a wife that works? That won't reflect well on them."

"Maybe Eliza isn't in a hurry to marry?" Rose suggested.

"If she's content to be a spinster, that's fine. But she's already twenty-two. There will be a new crop of eighteen-year-olds making their debut next season. It won't be as easy."

"I'm really not concerned with finding a husband," Eliza

said. Alice and Rose both looked horrified. Her grandmother seemed less shocked to hear it given their prior conversation.

"Getting married is a choice. Eliza doesn't need to rush into anything," their grandmother said.

"I just want to be really sure. To be head over heels in love," Eliza explained. "If I don't find that, at least I will be happy to have something to do."

"Well, that's a depressing thought. I am sure that getting married will make me happy. Being madly in love, well, that would be nice, too. But I think that could come, in time." Alice was very matter-of-fact about it all.

"What do you think, Rose? Are you anxious to marry?" Eliza asked.

Rose nodded. "I suppose that I am. It's what is expected, after all." She glanced at her sister and smiled. "I'd like to be in love first, too, though. I'm hopeful it will happen for all of us."

Their grandmother smiled. "I have every confidence that it will for you all, in time."

Eliza was glad to be back at the office, but throughout the week, she found herself missing Harry and thinking of him and his family often. She missed the camaraderie at the factory and she looked forward to seeing them at church on Sunday and for dinner after. She was eager to hear how their week went and if Harry had landed any new clients and orders.

When she got to the church, she saw that Harry and his family were already seated. Penny spotted her first and waved her over. Eliza noticed a pretty blonde woman sitting next to Harry. The woman seemed to know him well. Eliza watched with interest as the woman touched Harry's arm several times as she spoke and they both laughed at something she said. Penny noticed her looking.

"That's Angela, our cousin. She and Harry have always got on well."

Eliza relaxed a bit. That explained the familiarity.

"They're getting married!" Penny whispered dramatically.

Eliza froze. "But I thought you said they were cousins?"

"They are. Harry's helping her out." Penny didn't say more than that, but Eliza knew what she meant. Angela must be with child and for whatever reason, the father couldn't or wouldn't marry her. It was a noble thing to do, but Eliza thought it was a lot for Harry to sacrifice.

"When is the wedding?"

"There won't be a formal wedding. They're just going to marry at city hall, in a week or two."

"So soon!"

Penny nodded. "The sooner the better if Angela wants to avoid people talking."

Eliza glanced over at Harry again and this time he wasn't laughing. He met Eliza's gaze, and she saw the turmoil reflected there. Harry clearly didn't want to marry his cousin. She felt empty inside, as her hopes for what could be disappeared.

Eliza barely heard the service. It was all a blur. She stood whenever everyone stood and found the right hymns and mouthed the words as everyone sang around her. But she couldn't focus. And she couldn't look in Harry's direction again. She just wanted to go home. It was too painful to see him with someone else. Even if it was just his cousin. Even if it wasn't real. Getting married was real.

When the service ended and everyone went outside, Harry's mother gave her a hug. "You'll come to the house for Sunday dinner?"

But Eliza shook her head. "Thank you. But I'm not feeling well suddenly. I think it's best if I just head home."

"Oh, dear. Well, I hope you feel better."

Eliza said goodbye to the others and as she turned to leave, Harry and Angela walked out of the church together. Eliza felt hot tears spring up out of nowhere and wanted to get far away before they spilled over.

She only made it a few steps, though, before Harry was beside her. He was by himself. Angela had caught up with the others.

"You're not joining us? I was looking forward to seeing you. To catch up."

Eliza shook her head. "You're getting married. Now we're caught up."

She tried to keep the hurt out of her voice, but Harry heard it and took a step back.

"I had to. Angela, well, she's in a bad way."

"It's your life, Harry," Eliza said and sighed. "You're just giving up so much."

Harry stayed quiet for a moment, then ran his hand

through his hair and looked frustrated. "People marry for all kinds of reasons. I'm trying to do a good thing."

"I know. It's just, well, I thought..." Eliza sighed. "It doesn't matter what I thought. I hope you'll be happy, Harry." She turned to leave and felt Harry's hand on her arm.

"Eliza, we live in very different worlds. Your grandmother would never allow it. And I wouldn't do anything to hurt you." His voice broke, and she saw the truth in his eyes. He cared for her, too.

"I don't care what people think," she said defiantly.

His eyes softened, and he took her hand. "You should care. It does matter what people think. It's just the way things are. I hope we can still stay friends. Your friendship is important to me."

Eliza nodded. "Of course. But maybe not for a little while. It's too hard for me, and we both have to keep our focus."

He nodded. "I understand. And you're right. I hope your first week back in the office went well?"

She brightened a bit as the conversation shifted. "It did. It's good to be back. How was it for you?"

He grinned. "We got a second order from Macy's. The first sold out in only three days."

"Oh, that's wonderful news. I'm so happy for you, Harry."

"Thank you." He squeezed her hand and met her eyes, and they stayed like that for a long moment before he finally released her, and sighed. "I should probably go and catch up with the others. I hope to see you soon for Sunday dinner. You're always welcome, you know."

Eliza nodded and watched him walk off. She stood a few steps toward home and it wasn't long before the tears flowed fast and furious. Harry was getting married.

"Did your grandmother at least punish her in some way?" Miriam asked. She was helping Eliza dress for dinner later that evening and Eliza had no appetite whatsoever. Her mind was still spinning with Harry's news.

"Alice? Rose was the one that was truly sorry. Alice bullied her into going along with her scheme," Eliza said. "But Grandmother is making both of them go with her to all of her charity meetings this week and making them get involved. Alice and Rose will be serving the homeless supper in a soup kitchen every Sunday for the next three months. As you can imagine, Alice wasn't keen on the idea."

Miriam chuckled. "I would like to be a fly on the wall to see that. It will be good for them, though, to see beyond their world."

"I may go too," Eliza said.

"Don't you usually go to Harry's family's house after church?"

"I might not go for a while. Did you know Harry's getting married?"

The look of shock upon Miriam's face made it clear she did not know. Eliza told her about the upcoming marriage to his cousin.

"That's so nice of him. But, it is a sacrifice. There was no one Harry was interested in as far as I know, though. People get married like this all the time."

Eliza sighed. "I know. It's just. Well, it's Harry."

Miriam looked at her closely. "You're not keen on him for yourself?"

Eliza didn't say anything, just looked out the window, and felt miserable.

"Oh, Eliza. I didn't realize. Harry's a wonderful fellow. But, well, you know it's not done, right? Your cousins and your grandmother would be so upset. Mrs. Astor would never recognize him."

Eliza smiled. "I'm sure she wouldn't. Don't you think that's a bit silly, though? We do nothing to earn our place in society. It's just good luck to be born into it."

Miriam nodded. "I couldn't agree more. But that is how things are. There's not much we can do about it. Not unless you want to be ostracized. The invitations will stop coming."

"I'm not sure that would be such a bad thing," Eliza said with a wry smile.

"I know you think you wouldn't mind it, but it's important to keep up appearances. If you fall out of favor, you might find people taking their real estate business elsewhere."

Miriam made a good point. "I'm sure you're right. It doesn't matter much anymore anyway, since Harry is no longer available."

"What about that handsome Will? It seemed like he took such a shine to you?"

Eliza smiled. "Will is wonderful. A good friend, but he's not for me. I'm resigning myself to being a spinster. And I'm quite fine with the idea of it."

Miriam smiled. "I don't think you will be a spinster. Your season has been cut short now that you're in mourning, that's all. There's always next season."

But next season was the last thing on Eliza's mind. Still, she nodded. "I'm sure you're right."

As she made her way down to dinner, Eliza was already thinking about work. She intended to throw herself into the business even more than she had already. She wanted to learn everything and focus all her energy there, so she wouldn't have to think about Harry getting married to someone else.

34

For the next few weeks, Eliza immersed herself in work—learning everything possible about her father's business. She sat in on all meetings, listened, and took notes. She also studied all the business newspapers and visited Minnie several times, and learned more about the stock market as they chatted. Eliza had been following the railroads ever since Minnie first mentioned it to her, and she decided to invest a sizable amount of her inheritance in the market. Well, it seemed like a huge amount to her, but given the size of her overall inheritance, it was actually a modest sum—and she was curious and eager to enter the market with Minnie's guidance.

"If what I think is going to happen—we will soon have a strong demand for those shares and can resell them at a handsome profit." There was a gleam in Minnie's eye that Eliza now recognized when Minnie was particularly excited about an investment or new idea.

"I think so too. But I know it may take a while," Eliza said. Minnie always spoke about buying and holding and not being anxious for prices to rise.

Minnie nodded. "This might not take all that long. I think something is going to happen in the next month or two. There's a lot of activity right now.

Eliza headed back to the office after meeting with Minnie and sharing two turkey sandwiches that Eliza had brought in with her. Minnie was usually too busy to remember to pack a lunch, and Eliza thought it was the least she could do for taking so much of her time.

Everyone was heading into the conference room for their weekly status meeting as Eliza walked in, so she grabbed some paper to take notes and joined them. She'd kept an eye on the time, and made sure to be back in time for the meeting.

The meeting was fairly uneventful for the first half hour, as they all gave updates on current projects. But then John, one of the men who'd worked for her father for many years, said something that took her by surprise.

"I ran into Michael Sullivan at the Knickerbocker Club last night. He's very interested in the new property, and may want to buy a unit for his son as a wedding gift, possibly a penthouse."

Eliza recognized the name. Michael Sullivan was an acquaintance of her father's. He was one of his very wealthy friends.

"That's fantastic news," Richard said. "Especially as nothing is officially on offer yet. Word is getting out."

John smiled. "I may have planted the seed a few weeks ago over cocktails at the club."

"Which property is he referring to?" Eliza asked. As far as she knew, there were no new properties under development with penthouses that would be of interest to Michael Sullivan.

Richard met her gaze and matter-of-factly said, "The new development your uncle started working on before he passed."

Eliza looked around the room. "I'm confused. I thought that was to be affordable housing?"

Richard and John exchanged glances while the others stayed quiet.

"We decided to go in a different direction. There is a lot of demand from our affluent clientele for that location. It's just a business decision, what's best for the company," Richard said. The others all nodded in agreement.

"I see." Eliza wanted to scream and remind Richard that this was not what her father wanted. But she decided to wait until the meeting was over and speak to him privately, rather than embarrass him and cause the others to resent her.

The meeting continued, and Eliza held her tongue and jotted down notes as the others spoke. When the meeting adjourned, she followed Richard into his office and shut the door behind him.

He looked at her dismissively. "Is there something I can help you with?"

"I'd like to discuss the property that was supposed to be affordable housing."

Richard sighed. "I thought we settled that. I explained to you in the meeting that we are going in a different direction."

"That's not what my uncle wanted." Eliza crossed her arms and waited for him to respond.

"I'm trying to do what is best for the company. What is most profitable. Your uncle meant well, but affordable housing isn't the best use for that project."

"That decision was already made by my uncle. It's not up to you to change it," Eliza said quietly.

"It has already been changed, Eliza." He looked at her in frustration.

"Change it back. That property is to be all affordable housing. There is a huge need for it."

"It's not as profitable."

"That doesn't matter. This company is very profitable. My uncle wanted to also help the community. To do the right thing and to give back by building homes that the average person could afford. Nice homes. Not everyone in Manhattan is rich."

Eliza paused but Richard said nothing and sat at his desk, signifying that the conversation was over—the decision made. Which only infuriated Eliza further.

"Do I need to remind you of the terms of my uncle's will? He trusted me to carry on his vision—that's why he gave me the final say. No penthouses on this project. Affordable housing only. Are we clear on that?" Eliza spoke firmly and held his gaze, even though she felt wobbly inside.

He clearly wasn't happy about it, but after a long uncomfortable moment of silence, he nodded. "All right. Affordable housing, it is. I'll let the others know we're shifting back to the original plan."

Eliza smiled and relaxed a little. "Thank you, Richard."

She went back into her father's office and sat at his desk and found the plans her father had drawn up for the affordable housing units he wanted to build on that property. She looked through them and felt a sense of pride. Her father was a good man, who looked beyond his own profits to do something good. To build quality homes that were sorely needed by so many. During one of their drives, Harry had pointed out the awful tenement buildings that were barely livable but were the only thing many living in the city could afford. Soon, there would be more options. It was a start and if Eliza had her way, there would be more projects like this one.

35

*R*ose had a gleam in her eye when they all sat down to supper the next evening. Alice seemed excited too and Eliza hadn't any idea why. As soon as they were settled and the wine was poured, Rose held up her hand to show off a rather large diamond engagement ring.

"Paul proposed earlier today. And of course, I said yes!"

Their grandmother smiled and looked quite pleased. "That's wonderful, Rose. How soon would you like to marry?"

"Paul wants to do it as soon as possible. Neither of us really sees a reason to wait. But I suppose it takes some time to arrange a proper wedding. Would two months from now be too soon? We'd like to do it here in the city, since Alice is having hers in Newport."

It seemed awfully soon to Eliza. Especially as Alice and Nick were marrying in a little over a month. Though that wedding couldn't come soon enough for Eliza. Once they married, Alice would be moving in with Nick and soon after Rose's wedding, she would head to England with him and his family. Eliza felt a bit mean thinking it, but she really wouldn't miss Alice.

"I think we could manage that. I will check with the caterers tomorrow and let you know."

"Where will you and Paul live?" Alice asked.

"Yes, where will you live? You're both welcome to stay here. There's plenty of room," Grandmother offered.

"Thank you, but Paul wants us to move to Philadelphia. He has a house there, and it's where his business is located."

Grandmother looked disappointed, but nodded. "Philadelphia's not so far by train."

"It's really not! And of course we'll visit often," Rose said.

Eliza smiled to herself and reached for her wine. Now she truly was a spinster and would soon be living alone with her grandmother. And she didn't mind the thought of it at all. It would be quiet and peaceful. Though she knew her grandmother would much prefer if Rose and her new husband lived with them. But she also understood that it wasn't practical.

They were all heading to Newport in a few weeks for the summer. Eliza was curious to see it after hearing so much about it. And Alice couldn't stop talking about her wedding.

"It's going to be so gorgeous on the front lawn overlooking the ocean. Everyone who's anyone will be there," Alice said excitedly.

Eliza yawned. Alice's wedding would be just like the huge pretentious balls she'd been to. She wasn't looking forward to the wedding as much as seeing Newport itself and maybe swimming in the ocean. Rose had said the beaches there were lovely.

Later that evening, after Miriam helped Eliza dress for dinner, she retired for the evening and joined Colin at home. She collapsed on the sofa next to where he sat reading. He put his book down and she swung her legs onto his lap for her nightly foot rub. Colin kneaded the soles of her feet and she sighed with contentment.

"How was your day? Feeling all right?" Colin worried like a mother hen, but Miriam was feeling fine, just a bit tired. She told him so and filled him in on the latest news about the family.

"I passed Henry in the hallway as he was bringing in their next course, and he told me that Rose is engaged. So there are to be two weddings this summer."

"How will that affect us, do you think?" Colin asked.

"Well, they'll both be living elsewhere. But Eliza and her grandmother aren't going anywhere. So our jobs should be secure." They wouldn't be joining the rest of the family in Newport except on the weekends, as Eliza went into the office during the week.

"I wondered if Eliza might take the summer off and join the others in Newport?" Colin said.

"She loved working with her uncle and was happy to

return to the office. I think she'd go out of her mind if she was there all week with those two and nothing to do other than one party after the next."

"Right. Their mourning period will be over. I'm sure Rose, and especially Alice, are eager to resume their social engagements," Colin said.

Miriam chuckled. "That is an understatement. Alice has been miserable. She misses all the attention, and I know she's likely dying to show off her engagement ring."

"It will be quiet around here with those two gone. Peaceful." Colin smiled and pulled Miriam in for a kiss. "I like peaceful."

"So do I."

36

That Sunday, Eliza decided to go back to church, and if she was invited, to Harry's mother's house. She'd come to terms somewhat with the idea of Harry marrying his cousin and she didn't want to keep avoiding them all. She missed them, Harry especially—even if they could never be more than friends, she still valued his friendship.

So, she set off to church and this time Harry spotted her first and broke into a huge grin. He waved her over, and she slid into the pew next to him, just as the service started. She was surprised that Angela was nowhere in sight. They couldn't really talk until after the service, as the music began and everyone stood a moment later for the first hymn.

When the service ended and they walked outside, Harry spoke first. "You're coming to Sunday dinner, I hope?"

"Is that an invitation?" she teased.

"You're always invited. You know that."

"Please come," Penny said. "We've missed you."

"Of course I'll come. I was hoping you might ask."

Harry's mother came over and gave her a hug. "It's so good to see you. I had a feeling you might come today. I made extra meatballs."

Eliza floated along, basking in the love and laughter from Harry's family. She'd never experienced anything like it before. It had always just been herself and her mother and they'd shared a room in the Ashtons' mansion. They'd never had a home of their own and she'd always wondered what it might be like to have siblings. The relationship she had with Alice and Rose wasn't exactly what she'd had in mind. Though things were getting better with Rose, at least.

As they saw Harry's mother's house up ahead, Eliza asked about Angela. "Will she be joining us?"

Harry's eyes twinkled. "No, she's in Philadelphia."

"Oh, is she visiting family?"

"She's moved there, actually, with Alex."

Eliza stopped short. "You didn't marry?" She'd assumed they'd been married for several weeks now.

"We did not marry. Angela wrote to Alex to let him know about the wedding and he came to his senses and rushed here by train and took her home with him. I think he really does love her in his own way. It just took time for him to realize it. Too long, in my opinion, but she's happy. And so am I."

"Well, that is very good news for all of you," Eliza said.

Harry grinned. "I couldn't agree more." He held the door open when they reached the house and Eliza stepped inside and inhaled deeply. The soul-satisfying smell of rich tomato sauce and meat filled the room. They all piled into the kitchen and the girls helped Harry's mother dish out the pasta and meatballs. They gathered around the big round table and Penny poured small glasses of red wine for all of them.

Eliza spent the next few hours eating and laughing and listening as Harry and his family filled her in on everything she'd missed.

"The factory is humming along. We've picked up several big orders from the other major department stores. We're really on our way."

"Harry hired three more people to keep up with the work," Penny said proudly.

"That's fantastic. I'm so happy—for all of you."

After dinner, Eliza helped clear the table and then Harry's mother shooed them out of the kitchen. "I can finish up here. Harry, why don't you and Eliza go for a walk? It's a beautiful afternoon."

"I think that's a splendid idea." Harry nodded her way and Eliza smiled.

"I'd love to stretch my legs. I'm so full. Thank you. It was wonderful, as usual."

Harry led the way outside, and they strolled around the neighborhood. It was unusually warm for the time of year and felt like summer was close by. Eliza looked forward to the warmer weather. She told Harry that the family was getting ready to head to Newport soon.

He frowned at the news. "Will you go all summer, too?"

Eliza shook her head. "No. I'll go with them that first weekend, but I'll be back after that. I intend to keep working through the summer. My grandmother would love for me to join them every weekend, but I think that might be too far to go that often. I'll wait and see what I think, though. Maybe I will fall in love with Newport and feel anxious to get back there."

Harry laughed. "It is supposed to be beautiful. I've never been. Selfishly, though, I hope you don't fall in love with it too much. It was nice having you join us again. We all missed you." He held her eyes a moment longer than usual and Eliza felt a warm glow.

"I missed you all, too." They walked along and a moment later, she added, "You're lucky to have grown up in such a close family. I always wished for siblings."

Harry grinned. "Well, your wish came true....sort of."

Eliza laughed. "Rose is growing on me, but Alice is definitely not what I had in mind. It has been lovely getting to know my grandmother, though, and my father. I still can't believe he's gone already. I didn't have enough time with him."

"I know. We're never ready for them to leave us. My father's death was sudden too. Though of course it's not the same at all. I had a lifetime with him before that."

"I'm sure that was very hard for all of you," Eliza said softly. They walked along silently for a few moments before Harry pointed out a dilapidated building. "Can you believe people live there? The landlord refuses to make repairs and there are just not enough other affordable options for the tenants."

"It's awful. Shameful of those landlords. How do they get away with it?"

"Money talks. All these landlords are wealthy and have friends in the right places, so they look the other way."

"Well, in a year, maybe a bit less, there will be some other options for people in situations like this." Eliza told him about her conversation with Richard and Harry looked impressed.

"Good for you for holding your own. That's why your father made that change to his will. He knew he could count on you to carry out his vision."

They chatted easily for another hour or so as they walked along. Neither was in a hurry to rush home, but eventually they circled back to Harry's mother's house just as the sun was beginning to set. She had dessert waiting for them, a rich chocolate cake, and Eliza knew better than to protest. She ate cake with the others and sipped a cup of hot tea. It had been a lovely day, but she didn't want to overstay her welcome. So when they finished dessert, she said her goodbyes. And Harry insisted on driving her home.

"It's not safe to be walking that far after sunset."

Eliza gratefully accepted and was glad to spend a little more time in his company.

The ride was a short one though, and before she knew

it, Harry pulled into her driveway. He jumped out and opened her door, and she impulsively hugged him good-bye. At first he stiffened, but then hugged her back and held her tight for a moment. Eliza held her breath, hoping that maybe he might kiss her goodbye, but he didn't.

He pulled away a moment later, and she scolded herself for being so silly. Harry had made it clear that he just wanted to be friends and she understood and respected his reasoning, even if she didn't like it. And optimistically she couldn't help but think that if they spent more time together, at some later date, possibly he might come around.

"Goodnight, Harry."

"Goodnight. Will we see you next Sunday?"

She smiled. "It's quite possible."

Two weeks later, on a Friday, Eliza, Miriam and Colin took the train to Wickford, Rhode Island then rode a steamship for a little over an hour to Newport Harbor, where Ben was waiting with the carriage. Her grandmother, sisters, and most of the staff left the day before. Since Colin was staying behind for the summer to drive Eliza and be with Miriam, Ben, a senior footman, was filling in as a driver in Newport. It was still light when they arrived and Colin asked Ben to drive around for a bit so Eliza and Miriam could see the neighborhood.

As they rode along Bellevue Avenue, Colin pointed out the various homes by name—Rosecliff, The Elms, and Marble House took Eliza's breath away and then Ben turned onto Ochre Point Avenue and pointed out The Breakers. It was a home grander than anything Eliza had seen before.

"Cornelius Vanderbilt built The Breakers and his son

William and wife Alva built Marble house. I hear The Breakers is over sixty thousand square feet," Ben said.

"And they really call these mansions 'summer cottages'?" Eliza was stunned at the grandeur of it.

Ben laughed. "Well, George Vanderbilt, Cornelius's grandson, built a home in Asheville, NC that is almost three times this size. So, maybe to them it is."

"I truly can't imagine," Miriam said.

Ben pulled back onto Bellevue Avenue and rode down a bit further before turning into a long driveway. As they came around the curve, Eliza gasped at the beauty of the home before them. It wasn't as massive or as grand as The Breakers or Marble House, but it was still breathtaking. The house was an all-white, sprawling two-storied home with window boxes overflowing with dusty pink roses.

A sweeping, manicured lawn led to the home, which was situated at the water's edge overlooking the harbor. It was all ocean, for as long as Eliza could see. The air smelled crisp and clean, and she inhaled deeply. She hadn't even stepped inside and yet she could already understand the appeal of Newport. It was a magnificent and beautiful place.

Colin and Ben took the bags inside, and Eliza and Miriam followed them. They stepped into a large foyer, which opened into a huge living area with oversized bay windows that almost made it feel like the house was sitting on the water itself. The ceilings were high, Eliza guessed, eleven or twelve feet, which made the room seem even bigger. It was quiet and peaceful, though. Eliza wondered where her grandmother and sisters were.

Canning stepped into the room a moment later and informed them that everyone was at a neighbor's house for dinner. There was only a barebones staff left in the city now.

"I don't expect them back much before midnight," Canning said.

Miriam yawned at that and Eliza found herself doing the same. Miriam had packed sandwiches for them to eat on the train, and though it was early, she was ready to fall into bed. "Thank you, Canning. I think I'm going to retire. It has been a long day. I'm sure Miriam is tired as well?"

Miriam nodded.

"Very well. I'll let them know you'll see them in the morning. I'll show you to your room. Colin and Miriam are in the room at the very end of your hall."

Canning led the way and Eliza sighed with happiness when she stepped into the bedroom. It was spacious and cozy with soft silk bed coverings in a butter yellow shade and royal blue velvet draperies tied back with a pale-yellow silk cord. There were stunning ocean views from windows along two walls of the corner room. Tomorrow, after a good night's sleep, she could better appreciate it.

Miriam helped her to undress, and it didn't take long.

"Can I get you anything else?" Miriam asked. She looked like she was fighting back another yawn, and Eliza smiled.

"No, thank you. I'll see you in the morning. Sleep well."

The next day, while everyone else in the family slept in, Eliza rose early, had a light breakfast and ventured off to explore. Canning had explained earlier that there was a walking trail that went for several miles. There was no direct beach access from the house as it was high up and there were rocks below, which is how Cliff Walk got its name. Eliza set off along Cliff Walk until she reached Easton's Beach and took her shoes off. The water was cold, so she only dipped her toes in. But the sun was shining, and she took a long walk along the sandy shore before heading back to the house.

Her grandmother was up and sitting in the living room having coffee when Eliza returned.

"Your cheeks are rosy. Did you go all the way to Easton's Beach?"

Eliza gave her grandmother a hug and joined her on the sofa that faced the bay window overlooking the water.

"Yes, it's really breathtaking. I took in the views of the mansions—or should I call them 'cottages' as I walked."

Her grandmother laughed. "They all wanted to outdo each other. Your father never cared about that. He just wanted a comfortable, beautiful home on the water. Now, do you understand why we like to spend our summers here?"

Eliza nodded. "I do. The air smells different here. Saltier, cleaner somehow."

"We have a busy weekend planned. Alva Vanderbilt is throwing a party tonight to celebrate Alice and Nick's engagement."

Eliza was suitably impressed. "Really? At the Marble House? Alice must be thrilled."

"She is. Alva and Nick's mother are close friends. Her daughter, Consuelo, married Nick's mother's best friend's son."

Eliza laughed. "It really is a small world sometimes. Is the Marble House as beautiful inside as it is out? Ben drove us around a bit when we arrived."

"It's stunning. Too much marble for me, but I can still appreciate the splendor—it's quite the sight. And we are eating lightly for luncheon. Alva's dinners are decadent."

Eliza made a mental note to wear a dress that had a more forgiving waistline. She was looking forward to seeing Nick and congratulating him, too.

The interior of Marble House was even more opulent than Eliza could have imagined. There were stained glass windows, ornate carvings on the walls, moldings and ceilings, and so much marble. Many of the floors that were not marble were gleaming wood in an intricate herringbone pattern.

There were hundreds of guests in attendance, but the rooms were so big and the ceilings so high that it still felt airy and spacious instead of crowded. A string band played soft jazz in one corner of the ballroom, while tuxedo-clad waiters glided by offering hot appetizers or glasses of champagne.

Just before they were to sit down for dinner, Eliza saw Nick, and he waved and came right over to say hello.

"Congratulations on your engagement. Alice is so excited."

Nick grinned. "Thank you. Alice and I have fun. I think it will be a good marriage." She noticed that he didn't mention being madly in love, but she supposed perhaps that was assumed. He certainly seemed enthusiastic enough.

They chatted for a few more minutes, then went to find their seats for dinner. Eliza was seated next to her grandmother and a man she didn't recognize. He introduced himself as Peter Thompson. She guessed that he was in his late thirties or early forties. He was slightly balding and as they chatted through dinner, she learned that he was a widow and that he also worked in real estate. He also expressed his condolences.

"I knew your uncle well. We did several deals together a number of years ago. I think we both hoped to have the opportunity to work together again at some point. I don't know how familiar you are with your uncle's business?"

Eliza explained that she was very involved and familiar with her father's past projects. As soon as he told her his name, and that he worked in real estate, she'd immediately pulled up his file in her mind.

"Your projects both included a sizable affordable housing component, if I recall?"

He looked impressed. "Yes. That was important to both of us. I was actually thinking to get in touch with him about a project I'm considering, to see if he might want to partner with me, like we did in the past." He smiled sadly.

"I'm afraid my timing was unfortunate. I would have loved to work with him again. I thought of him as I heard about his newest project."

"What did you have in mind?" Eliza was intrigued.

He grinned. "It's a project that might infuriate some. And that appeals to me. It's a stretch of Madison Avenue that is quite near some of the more expensive mansions. What I envision is a mixed-use building, half of it luxury units, beautiful penthouse apartments but also smaller, more affordable homes, too. A chance for those of modest means to live in a nicer neighborhood. I know not everyone will admire that idea."

Eliza loved the concept and told him so. "I think my uncle would have loved this idea. I know I do. What would you need from us to partner with you?"

He discussed the details of what he had in mind as they ate and Eliza wanted to immediately say yes, but knew she needed to discuss with the team in the office to make sure they had the resources to take the project on. And she suspected they might not be as enthusiastic about the affordable price point on some of the units. But the price that Peter mentioned sounded incredibly good to her.

"I've been sitting on this land for some time now, and I got a deal on it at the time. I just don't have the capacity at the moment to take on the entire project, which is why I thought of your uncle."

"I would love to do it with you. I'll discuss with the others in my office on Monday when I return and will let you know as soon as possible."

"Wonderful! I'm so glad I decided to come to this event. I almost didn't you know. I wasn't feeling entirely festive as it has only been a few months since I lost Doris and I knew that your uncle wouldn't be attending. I am so glad that you are carrying on his work."

After dinner, the dancing began, and Eliza was happy to move around and enjoy the music. She danced with Peter and many of the other men in attendance, except, of course, for Nick. During a break, while sipping a glass of water and leaning against the cool marble wall, Eliza watched the crowd and overheard something that concerned her.

Two men she recognized as friends of Nick's stood nearby, watching the crowd and commenting on the guests. They seemed to know everyone and had an opinion about them all. When Nick and Alice whirled by one of them snickered.

"Lucky duck. He got what he came here for—soon to be married to one of the richest heiresses in the Manhattan."

"He looks happy enough? Maybe there's a true love match there?"

His friend scoffed. "I doubt it. Nick's goal was to catch a rich heiress, and he outdid himself. He loves her money, that much I'm sure of. Once they're settled back in England, he'll be free to do whatever he wants—pursue whoever he wants."

"She's a pretty girl, though."

"Sure, she's attractive enough. But now he has options.

And I'm sure his parents are thrilled. He told me their country estate is badly in need of repair."

Eliza frowned. She'd heard the rumors that Nick was hoping to marry an heiress, but she hadn't fully believed them or knew that his family was having money issues. She debated whether to share what she'd heard with Alice. And then she immediately decided against that idea. Alice wouldn't welcome it and probably wouldn't believe Eliza if the information came directly from her.

As she was debating whether to tell Rose, she suddenly appeared by her side.

"What are you doing standing here like a wallflower? You should be dancing," Rose said.

"I was just taking a break. I just overheard something though and was deciding whether or not to tell you—as it concerns Alice."

Rose looked intrigued. "Why not just tell Alice?"

"I don't think she would want to hear it from me, frankly."

Rose nodded. "You're probably right. Now that you've mentioned it, though, you must tell me."

Eliza repeated everything she'd heard and waited for a reaction from Rose.

"I won't be saying anything to Alice about this."

That shocked Eliza. "No? Why not? You don't think she should know before she marries him?"

Rose smiled. "She already knows this. Alice knows exactly what she's getting with Nick. A title and fun times. She's hopeful he might learn to love her, but she still feels like she's getting a good deal with this marriage. She thinks having a title will elevate her in society and she's looking forward to the adventure of living in London."

"Oh, all right, then. As long as she's happy."

"I've never seen her this happy."

38

A few minutes after Eliza arrived at work on Monday, she had a surprise visitor. Minnie knocked lightly on her office door and Eliza laughed when she saw her.

"Come in! This is a nice surprise. Have a seat." She noticed Minnie had a familiar gleam in her eye.

Minnie settled into one of the two chairs facing Eliza's desk. "I have some very good news for us. You know that Georgia Central stock we bought at $70 a share a while back?"

Eliza nodded. It was the railroad stock and her first big purchase. Though her stake was small compared to the more than six thousand shares that Minnie had accumulated.

"Well, Friday afternoon, two officers from Richmond Terminal Railroad paid me a visit at the bank. They're looking to take control of Georgia Central and they made me an offer on my stock. It wasn't enough of course—They only offered $100."

"You didn't accept?" Eliza mentally did the math in her head. The amount of potential profit was staggering.

Minnie laughed. "I never accept a first offer. They can always do better. We went back and forth a bit and I got them up to $127.50. And I told them I could include your shares at the same price."

Eliza had bought exactly one hundred shares. It was a tiny fraction of the amount that Minnie owned, but to Eliza, it seemed like an enormous amount of money. She'd paid seven thousand dollars for her shares of Georgia Central and now they were worth $5750 more than she'd paid for them.

"That's incredible."

Minnie grinned. "I'm glad you're excited because I told them yes on your behalf. And I brought you a document to sign confirming the sale. Once you sign here, it's official."

Eliza quickly signed and couldn't stop smiling. It didn't seem real.

"So, how was Newport? Did you have fun?" Minnie asked.

Eliza told her all about her weekend and they chatted a few minutes longer, before Minnie said goodbye and headed back to Chemical Bank.

Twenty minutes later, Eliza joined the others in the conference room for the start of their weekly meeting.

"You're looking unusually happy," John said as Eliza sat

down. "Did you love Newport? Will you leave us now and spend the rest of the summer there?" he teased.

Eliza laughed. "Newport was fun. But what I'm more excited about was that I just had my first big win with the stock market."

"Is that why Minnie Greene was here? I didn't realize the two of you were friends. What is she investing in now?" John leaned forward and the rest of the men looked equally intrigued.

"Richmond Terminal Railroad is looking to gain control of Georgia Central and Minnie and I just sold our shares to them."

"At a nice profit, I imagine?" John looked impressed.

"Yes, Minnie did most of the work on this. I've learned a lot from her."

"Congratulations. She's quite the investor. I've been hearing her name a lot lately," John said.

"Well, shall we move on to the weekly updates? Who wants to go first?" Richard asked.

Once everyone had discussed the status of current projects, Richard asked if there was any new business to discuss. No one else spoke up, so Eliza told them about the project Peter spoke about at dinner.

"I know my uncle would have loved this project, and I was tempted to tell him yes, but I didn't want to do that until I spoke to all of you first. I wanted to make sure we have the resources to take this on."

The room was silent for a moment and then John spoke. "We've worked with Peter several times before. He's a good partner. And I think we can put the resources together for this."

Richard nodded. "Just to clarify, Peter wishes for this Madison Avenue development, in one of the most exclusive areas of the city, to be an equal mix of high-end units, penthouses even, and affordable housing?"

Eliza worried that he would hate the idea, but hoped anyway that he might still support it. "Yes, Peter says his other two projects with this company were both affordable housing developments and he wishes that to continue. It's important to him, as it was to my uncle."

Richard smiled and Eliza breathed a sigh of relief. She could see the acceptance in his eyes. "This will be a good project for us—even if half of it is affordable housing. It will be profitable and it may lead to other worthy projects. You may let Peter know that we look forward to working with him."

"I'll draft a letter to him today. Thank you." She looked around the table. "Thank you, all of you. I know I'm new to working here, but I hope you are starting to understand how important this is to me and how much I love it?" Though she'd never be able to fully explain to them why she was so passionate about being in a position to make a difference with the affordable housing projects. Eliza didn't take her good luck for granted. She wanted to do something to help, to give back now that she'd fallen into an embarrassment of riches. She felt it was the least she could do.

39

Two months later, a week after Alice's wedding in Newport, Eliza went to church on Sunday and to dinner at Harry's mother's house. She'd fallen into a routine of going most Sundays aside from Rose's wedding a few weeks earlier. Newport was lovely, but it was just too far to go every weekend. And truth be told, she looked forward to Sundays with Harry and his family.

Over a delicious roast beef dinner, Eliza told them all about Alice's wedding.

"It was really beautiful. The weather was perfect, and they had the reception on the front lawn. There was so much food and the cake was heavenly."

"Was it very fancy?" Penny asked.

Eliza laughed. "It really was. Even though it was outside. There were massive tents, and lots of champagne and a wonderful band. Everyone danced all night."

"I bet the dresses were beautiful," Connie said.

"They were very pretty," Eliza agreed.

"Was it fancier than Rose's wedding?" Penny asked.

Eliza thought about that a moment. "It was just different. Rose's was a bit more formal, possibly as it was inside and it was a bit smaller, too. But also lovely."

"And they've both gone now? So it's just you in that big house?" Harry's mother asked.

"Yes. It's quiet now. But Grandmother is back. She didn't want to stay in Newport alone, and I'm glad to have her company." She'd grown used to the quiet with Rose and Alice gone all summer, but it was definitely nicer now that her grandmother was back. Eliza liked having her all to herself. They had long interesting discussions at dinner as her grandmother loved to hear about what they were working on at the office and shared her opinions, which Eliza valued.

After dinner, Harry and Eliza went for their usual walk around the neighborhood. She sensed that he had something he wanted to discuss and she could tell that whatever it was, he was excited about it. As soon as they stepped outside, he shared his news.

"I didn't want to say anything in front of the others yet, because I don't know if this will happen and I don't want to get their hopes up. I wanted to ask your advice, as I know you have several new projects in the area."

"What is it?" Eliza thought maybe he was excited about a new store or huge order, but the mention of real estate was unexpected.

"One of my suppliers let me know that a store is

coming available to lease on Madison Avenue. It's a factory and textile showroom right now and they are moving to a bigger location in the garment district."

"You want to move your factory there?" It seemed a bit soon to Eliza, but maybe he needed the room.

Harry grinned. "No. The factory is fine where it is. I want to open my department store there. The size is perfect. It just needs a bit of sprucing up, a nice coat of paint and some fresh flowers. And lots of clothing, of course."

"Well, that's wonderful. It sounds expensive, though." She wondered how much money Harry would need to do something like that.

"It is expensive. But I had a meeting with my investors just last week, before I heard about this opportunity, and they're encouraged by how well the factory is doing. We're ahead of projections. And they know about my long-term plans to open a department store." He grinned. "They told me to keep an eye out for a location and that they'd be willing to help. And then this came along. It really seems meant to be."

"It does. It's exciting. How long would it take to get the store ready to open?"

"Three to four months, I think. It will be available in two weeks, so we can start right away to get it cleaned up and painted and I can place our initial orders."

"So, what did you want to ask me? How can I help?"

"I just wanted to tell you. To see if you thought it was a good idea or if I'm crazy to try to do this so soon?"

"Do you feel like you're ready for it?"

"I do. I can't wait to get started. The location is perfect. It's a great area. And it's just a few blocks away from your two new developments. Those new tenants will need to shop."

Eliza laughed. "Yes, they will. I think you should do it, Harry. It's what you've always dreamed of and the opportunity came to you—it seems like it is meant to be."

Harry pulled her in for a quick, enthusiastic hug. "Good, because I've never been so excited about anything before." His eyes locked on hers and she held her breath for a moment. There was such a strong feeling in the air between them that she half-expected him to kiss her. But he didn't. Instead, he pulled away, and the moment was gone. They walked back slowly, talking non-stop the whole way. They'd become closer these past few months, and there was no shortage of things to discuss. Harry had quickly become her best friend, and she was grateful for his friendship, even while she wished it could be something more.

40

A little over three months later, on a sunny Saturday afternoon, Colin drove Eliza and Miriam to Harry's grand opening of Ford's department store. Eliza couldn't wait to see it, as she'd been hearing all about it every Sunday for weeks now. She could almost picture it in her mind, as Harry had detailed everything that would be on display.

Miriam shifted a bit in her seat as they rode. Eliza knew she was at the uncomfortable stage of her pregnancy. She was due in a little over a week, and her stomach was big and round. She and Colin were anxious and excited about the arrival of their first child.

"Have you decided on names, yet?" Eliza asked, as they rode along.

"We are close. I like Sophie or Anna if it's a girl and Colin really likes Liam if it's a boy."

Eliza glanced out the window and as they turned onto Madison Avenue, in the distance, she could see Harry's store and a long line waiting outside, which seemed like a good sign. There was a lot of excitement around this grand opening. As Colin pulled up to the store, the front door opened and the crowd of people swarmed inside. A moment later, Eliza, Miriam, and Colin joined them.

Harry stood at the door to greet everyone as they arrived. He was dressed in his best suit and wore the biggest smile Eliza had ever seen.

"I'm so glad you're all here. Come in and look around. Let me know what you think."

They stepped inside and Eliza stopped short to take in her surroundings. Near the entrance, a man played jazz music on a grand piano, which added to the festivity. Straight ahead was a counter with perfumes and shop girls smiling and squirting samples of the scents on ladies' wrists. The women's clothing was on the first floor and was the first thing they saw as they walked around the room. Elegant cloaks, dresses, hats, and shoes were artfully displayed. Men's clothing was on the second floor and Colin went to explore while Eliza and Miriam browsed the first level.

Eliza reached out and touched one of the dresses and smiled. The fabric was soft and silky to the touch, and of the highest quality. She peeked at the price tag and, while not inexpensive, she thought the price was reasonable, given the level of quality. Apparently, many women agreed as she saw a line quickly form for the dressing rooms in the back corner of the store.

"So, what do you think?" Harry appeared by her side, his eyes twinkling with excitement.

"It's marvelous, Harry. I'm so happy for you and proud of you!"

"Thank you. As you know, it's a dream come true." He glanced around the room, his enthusiasm dimming for just a second as he added, "Hopefully the customers will like it."

"Harry, look at the lines for the dressing room. I don't think you need to worry about that."

He grinned. "I sure hope you're right. I should probably head back to my post."

He wandered off to greet more new customers, and Eliza and Miriam continued to shop. The store grew more crowded and Eliza didn't want to stay too long because of Miriam's condition. She knew how easily Miriam tired now. They both made small purchases, though. Miriam bought a pair of baby socks and pajamas and Eliza found a cranberry-colored hat and matching gloves that were perfect for the cool fall weather. Colin didn't buy anything, but was impressed with the offerings for men.

They said goodbye to Harry and made their way out of the store, which now had a line of customers waiting to enter—it was so crowded inside now that they had to wait until people left to let others inside.

Colin led them to their carriage and helped Miriam into the passenger side while Eliza climbed in easily herself. Normally Colin would help her first, but Eliza insisted it wasn't necessary and his wife needed the help more. Once they were settled, Colin set off for home.

They'd only gone a few blocks when the unthinkable happened. A delivery truck with a team of horses going much too fast took a corner and the truck slammed into their carriage, knocking it over. The force of the collision opened Eliza's door and tossed her into the street. Miriam let out a piercing scream just before Eliza hit the ground hard and everything went totally black.

Eliza was confused and disoriented when she woke in an unfamiliar bed. The first thing she noticed was the antiseptic smell of the hospital. The second that her head and leg both throbbed with a dull pain. And then she noticed there were two people in the room with her and one of them was holding her hand. She looked up into Harry's worried eyes. He smiled with relief as she recognized him, and he gave her hand a reassuring squeeze.

"You're in the hospital. Do you remember what happened?" He asked.

Eliza glanced at the other figure in the room. Her grandmother sat on the opposite side of the bed and looked just as concerned.

"I was in the carriage on my way home with Miriam. Colin was driving us. Are they okay?"

"They're both fine," her grandmother assured her. "Colin was just bruised up a bit and Miriam was, of course, taken into the hospital as well. She's actually in labor right now and the doctor said everything looks as it should. She was safe in the carriage."

"You broke your leg," Harry explained. "When you were thrown from the carriage, you landed hard. The doctor thinks it should heal quickly, though. You will be on crutches for a while though, and you need to rest up and take it easy for a while."

Eliza nodded. "My leg does hurt a bit," she said just as the doctor walked over to them.

"I imagine it does. We'll give you something to help with the pain. You'll need to keep weight off that leg for about six weeks to allow it to heal properly. I'll send a nurse in with some pain medicine and crutches for you, and then you can go home."

"Harry, if you wouldn't mind giving us a lift home?" Eliza's grandmother asked. "I would like Ben to stay to drive Colin home once Miriam delivers her baby. She'll have to stay a few days, I'm sure."

"Of course I will."

Once the nurse returned with pain medication and a pair of crutches for Eliza, Harry and Eliza's grandmother walked on either side of her as she slowly maneuvered her way out of the hospital and into Harry's carriage. They made sure she made it safely into the house, and then Harry said goodnight.

"Eliza, I'll come by tomorrow to check on you. Sleep well."

Eliza just nodded. The pain medication was working, and she was eager to go to sleep. Canning and Mrs. Smith were waiting by the door when they arrived, and both looked relieved when they saw Eliza on her crutches.

"We thought it might be easier for Eliza to have a room on the ground floor until her leg heals," Canning said.

"It's ready for her. I put fresh sheets on the bed and there's a pitcher of water and the book she's been reading on her nightstand. If you come this way, Miss Eliza, I can help you get undressed and into bed. I brought some of your dresses and night clothes down from your room, as well."

"Thank you ever so much, both of you," Eliza's grandmother said.

Eliza smiled her gratitude at both of them. "Thank you," she said softly. It felt like such an effort to speak.

"Let's get you to bed, my dear. All will seem better in the morning," her grandmother said.

And she was right. When Eliza woke the next day, her leg still hurt, but she was grateful that it hadn't been worse. Mrs. Smith helped her to dress, and then Eliza hobbled into the dining room for breakfast. To her surprise, her grandmother was already there, sipping coffee and reading a newspaper. An untouched piece of toast sat in front of her. She looked up when Eliza walked in.

"Good morning, dear. Did you sleep well?"

Eliza carefully sat in the chair next to her grandmother and leaned her crutches against the adjacent seat. "I did, thank you. I don't actually recall the last time I slept so late. I suppose I needed it." Eliza was usually up early and at breakfast before eight. It was a few minutes past nine already.

Her grandmother smiled. "It's a good thing today is

Sunday, or I imagine you'd be looking for a ride into your office?"

Eliza laughed. "Probably so. I'm planning to go in tomorrow. I can rest just as easily there as I can here."

Her grandmother nodded. "And it will keep your mind busy."

"I'd be bored just sitting around."

"Yes, and that's why I agreed to Harry's suggestion to come get you for church today and your usual Sunday dinner with his family."

"You don't mind if I go?" Eliza hated to leave her grandmother alone and go off to eat with Harry's family.

Her grandmother shook her head. "I don't mind at all. Harry actually invited me to join them whenever I like. Which was kind of him. I told him I might take him up on that offer, but not today. And I know I'll be seeing you later this evening for dinner, as usual."

"Yes, of course you will."

Eliza's eggs and toast arrived a moment later, and she and her grandmother chatted as they ate. Her grandmother finally picked up her toast once she'd spread a thick layer of raspberry jam on it.

"You're not usually up for breakfast," Eliza commented as her grandmother polished off her last bite of toast.

"No, not usually. I suppose I wanted to check on you and make sure you were feeling better." There was a twinkle in her grandmother's eye that Eliza hadn't seen before, but it reminded her of Minnie's look when she was excited about something. Whatever was her grandmother up to?

"Oh, look who's here to collect you for church," her grandmother said as Harry walked into the room. "If you'd both excuse me, I need to go talk to Mrs. Shelby about tonight's dinner." Her grandmother disappeared from the room as Harry walked over and sat across from her at the table. Eliza took her last bite of eggs and washed it down with a sip of coffee.

"How are you feeling?" His eyes were full of warmth and concern.

She smiled. "Much better now that you're here. Grandmother says you're going to escort me to church and to Sunday dinner with your family."

"Yes. And I'm glad you're more awake now than you were last night. I wanted to have this conversation then. It was hard for me to wait. But I needed you to be in your right mind, and fully aware."

"Whatever are you talking about, Harry?"

"Well, while you slept in the hospital, your grandmother and I spoke for several hours. Idle chitchat at first, but then our conversation grew more serious. I asked her advice, and she considered it carefully and offered a solution that, well, I'm quite excited about and I think you will be, too. At least I hope you will be." He looked a bit nervous as he stood and then bent down onto one knee and pulled a dark brown velvet box from his pocket.

"Eliza, I've been carrying this for months. I didn't know if the right moment would ever come, but I knew this is what I wanted and I think what you wanted too. But I was serious about my reason for wanting to wait. I didn't want to jeopardize your business or your relationship with your grandmother."

Eliza's heart skipped a beat. Could what she'd dreamed of for so long finally happen?

Harry smiled. "Your grandmother actually brought the subject up first. I think she could see how I felt about you and she suspected how you feel about me since you didn't go to Newport every weekend like she'd hoped and instead spent your Sundays with me and my family. Which made us all very happy. My family adores you—they love you as part of the family, and Eliza I love you, too. I don't want to just see you on Sunday. I want to spend every day with you and every night and to grow old with you. Will you marry me?"

Tears of pure happiness spilled down Eliza's face. She brushed them away and took his hand. "Yes, of course I will. I love you, too, Harry. With all my heart. Now and for always."

Harry grinned. "I hoped you'd say that." He opened the small box and Eliza gasped at the beauty of the ring inside it. "This was my grandmother's ring. I added these small diamonds around the original diamond. Do you like it?"

The ring was stunning. The circle of smaller diamonds around the center diamond gave it a glittering halo effect, and the setting was a delicate platinum filigree. "I love it."

Harry slid the ring onto her finger and she sighed with

happiness. It fit perfectly. "I think I might just stare at this all day," she said.

Harry laughed. "I'm glad you like it."

"So, is it safe to come in now? Can we celebrate?" Eliza's grandmother peeked in the room, and Harry waved her over.

"She said yes!" He said proudly.

"Of course she did. Let's see the ring," her grandmother demanded.

Eliza held it up and her grandmother bent over to take a closer look. "Well, done, Harry. It's quite lovely. And congratulations, Eliza. I'm very happy for the both of you."

"Thank you. Harry said he spoke with you last night and you gave your blessing." Eliza was still quite in shock over the development, which was completely unexpected.

"Yes. I did. Harry was quite convincing, and I've always liked him. And I am impressed with what he has accomplished."

Harry turned to her and she saw the depth of love in his eyes. "When I got word that you'd been hurt, it was the worst feeling imaginable. I raced to the hospital, and I didn't know what I would do if you weren't in my life. I realized that it was time to accept that we need to be together, even if not everyone approves."

"Fortunately, I approve. And if I give my blessing, others will fall in line as well. And if they don't, well, that's their loss," her grandmother said. She went on to further explain, "At my age, you begin to realize that life is short and if you have the opportunity to find love, a love that is real and that will last, you'd be foolish not to pursue it." She smiled. "Although I did have one request of Harry."

Harry grinned. "Your grandmother would like us to live with her."

Eliza looked surprised. "You would? Really?"

"Yes, my dear. We've only just begun to know each other and there are many years ahead. There's plenty of room here. The two of you can have your own wing for privacy. With Alice and Rose gone, this house will feel awfully empty if it's just me and the staff. I hope you will consider it. It also shows my approval as well."

Eliza smiled. "I'd love to stay here, if Harry agrees."

"Whatever you want is fine by me." Harry nodded toward her grandmother. "I appreciate the offer and we gratefully accept."

"Good. From a practical perspective, it's also smart financially as it will eliminate a housing expense and perhaps help you to pay off your investors sooner," her grandmother added. "Well, now that we've settled that, I will get out of your way so the two of you can go off and celebrate properly."

Eliza hugged her grandmother goodbye and before she could reach for her crutches, Harry was by her side. "I think there's one more thing we need to do." He leaned in and pressed his lips to hers and she marveled at the feel of his lips on hers and wrapped her arms around his neck and pulled him close. Kissing Harry was even better than she'd imagined.

She would have loved if the kiss went on forever, but

they had to end it to make it to church on time. Harry helped her up and onto her crutches. As he walked beside her and held the door open, she saw his love reflected in his eyes and felt a new sense of peace and happiness. With Harry by her side, she looked forward to the rest of their life together.

EPILOGUE

CHRISTMAS EVE A LITTLE OVER A YEAR LATER

*E*liza sighed with happiness as she surveyed the living room. She and Harry had been married for a little over a year and were at his mother's house for Christmas Eve. There was a full, decorated tree in the corner of the living room, next to the fireplace. The room was bursting with people. Harry's whole family was there, as well as Eliza's grandmother, who was sitting in a leather armchair, sipping a Manhattan cocktail that Harry had just mixed for her.

Eliza had come earlier in the day and helped with the traditional holiday ravioli making. Harry spent the day in the store, though they closed a bit early, at four in the afternoon, so his employees could spend Christmas Eve with their families. Eliza took a sip of warm apple cider and patted her stomach. She'd only just felt the baby move for the first time a few days ago and Harry had been so excited when she called him over and placed his hand on her stomach so he could feel it, too. She was just over four months along and was feeling much more energetic. She'd been so sleepy and a bit nauseous for the first few months and was glad that seemed to be behind her.

"You look wonderful," Miriam said as she settled baby Sophie on her lap. Sophie was just over a year old and toddling everywhere. Miriam kept a sharp eye on her so she wouldn't get underfoot. Sophie yawned and looked ready for a nap. "If all goes well, I'll put her down to sleep just before we sit down to dinner."

Eliza smiled. "That sounds like a good plan. And thank you. I'm feeling so much better now."

"Once I got past month four, it was pretty smooth sailing the rest of the way. My appetite kicked in even more then."

Eliza laughed. "It certainly has. I'm looking forward to a second helping of ravioli already. How are you liking the Redfield apartment?"

Eliza was excited that Miriam and Colin were among the first residents to move into the affordable housing development that her father had begun just before his death. Harry had introduced Colin to a friend that was looking for a business partner and the two of them had teamed up to open a carriage repair shop. Colin had always loved maintaining the carriages and Miriam convinced him to make a business of it and it was going very well.

Miriam helped by handling the books and scheduling. Eliza missed seeing her every day, but she was excited about this opportunity for them both.

"We love it. It's lovely to have our own place. You must come soon for tea, to see it."

"I look forward to it."

Harry's mother stepped into the room and told everyone that it was time to gather around the table. They all found a seat and helped themselves to ravioli from one of the two huge platters in the middle of the table. Penny poured wine for those who wanted it, and Connie passed grated parmesan cheese around the table. Once everyone had a full plate, Harry's mother looked around the table and smiled. "I'm so grateful to have all of you here today. We are truly blessed with good friends and family." She glanced at Eliza, "and a new grandchild on the way." Everyone lifted their glasses in a toast of appreciation.

Eliza's grandmother sat on her right and Eliza smiled when she caught her eye. "I'm so glad you're here with us."

"How could I miss it? You've been raving about this ravioli forever, it seems." She took a bite, closed her eyes for a moment, and smiled. "And with good reason, I see. I'm thrilled to be here. And even more excited to be a great-grandmother soon."

Eliza turned her attention to Harry, who sat to her left. He glanced at the sofa, where baby Sophie lay sleeping peacefully under a soft blanket. "Next Christmas, Harry junior will be beside her."

Eliza laughed, "Or Vivian." If it was a girl, Eliza wanted to name her after her mother.

"Of course." He held Eliza's gaze for a moment, then spoke softly so only she could hear, "Are you as happy as I am?" His eyes glowed with love.

"I don't think I could possibly be any happier. Life is good, Harry."

"That it is. Merry Christmas, Eliza."

Thank you so much for reading Gilded Girl. I hope you enjoyed reading Eliza's story as much as I enjoyed writing it. =)

*** *Author's Note—When my sister read an early draft of this she questioned me about the stock prices that Minnie and Eliza paid—"Are you sure they really paid that much? $70 and $127.50 sounds like today's prices." And she was surprised when I told her that was accurate. Minnie Greene is based on a real woman, Hetty Green, who was a brilliant investor and actually made that very deal, as described. She was like a female Warren Buffett. I was so fascinated reading about her, that I thought it would be fun to have a similar character in this story.*

If you like to cook, please take a look at the recipe at the end of the book, for my Nana's ravioli which were the inspiration for Harry's mother's ravioli—so delicious.

The preorder for my Summer of 2023 book is now up. You can preorder Bookshop by the Bay, which is published by St. Martin's Press in paperback, hardcover or ebook. Audio will follow. I'm excited for you to read this story, which is set on Cape Cod, MA, where I grew up. It's set in the town of Chatham, which reminds me a bit of Nantucket....it's a more affluent area, with gorgeous waterfront homes, a picturesque Main Street, and lots of seals and great white sharks!

If you would like an email when I have a new release, please sign up here.

The story is about two fifty something best friends and their thirty-year-old daughters in a summer of change, and new possibilities as they chase their dream of running a bookshop together. =)

In the meantime, please also explore my other books, The Nantucket Inn series, The Restaurant books and The Hotel are all set on Nantucket. I've also written a few mysteries, most recently, Plymouth Undercover, which is set in my current hometown of Plymouth and features a mother and daughter team and their eighty-year-old part-time employee, a retired police detective.

I also have a very active and friendly Facebook group that you are welcome to join—the Pamela Kelley Reader group.

Thank you for spending your time with my stories. I appreciate it so much. ~Pam

NANA'S RAVIOLI

One of my grandmothers was Italian and every Easter and Christmas, Nana and Grandpa made the ravioli. It's difficult to put into words how good this is. Everything is homemade—from the pasta dough to the filling—which for some unknown reason is called 'the ping'.

Leftover ping is delicious baked in peppers or mushrooms. The filling itself takes time to make—one of the cheeses, American that you buy at a supermarket deli, needs to dry out in the refrigerator for three weeks so it will grate properly and have the right flavor. Seems odd, but trust me, it's worth it. This is the ravioli I grew up with, that is so rich and delicious and melts in your mouth. It has spoiled me for all other ravioli.

And I can still picture Nana and Grandpa in the kitchen, which would always look a disaster, with flour everywhere. My grandfather had a special extra door in the garage that he brought into the kitchen and set over two chairs and covered with a sheet, to make an extra work surface to lay the hundreds of ravioli, to dry out a little as they waited their turn to either be cooked or go into the freezer. They freeze really well.

So, here is the recipe. It makes a LOT, so feel free to cut in half or even a third. Enjoy. =) Special thank you to my Aunt Dianne, and my cousin Dana Claughton Volungis for sharing their updates on this recipe. They make it more often than I do!

Ingredients

16 large eggs

3 packages of cream cheese, 8 oz each room temp

36-44 breakfast sausage links—she liked Sunnyland, cooked and crumbled—or 2, 1 pound cooked and drained, Jimmy Dean bulk sausage rolls

3 packages frozen chopped spinach, 10 oz each

3 cups grated American cheese—buy a block from deli

1/2 pound grated Parmesan cheese

Dry American cheese in the refrigerator for about 3 weeks, unwrapped. Then grate. Squeeze water out of cooked, cooled spinach. Mix the room temp cream cheese, and cooked sausage. Add spinach to a food processor and chop finely, add sausage and cream cheese and eggs, working in batches of about 1/3 at a time, until well blended. Put in a large mixing bowl and stir in grated cheeses. Cover and let rest overnight—will dry out some and firm up.

Dough--a two pound bag—we like the Italian flour,

Antimo Caputo brand. But King Arthur or Pillsbury is fine, too. In a large bowl, add flour. Mix two tablespoons salt (we like pink Himalayan, but any salt is fine) with three cups warm water. Slowly add water to flour, mixing into a smooth dough ball. Let rest for 30 minutes.

Flour a surface, and using a rolling pin, roll out the dough a section at a time—pinch off a smaller ball and then roll to a thin sheet. Using a teaspoon, drop a rounded amount evenly across the dough—about two inches apart. Top with a similar size sheet. Using a ravioli rolling pin— or just a knife, cut the ravioli and press down on the edges. Continue making the ravioli until you run out of dough or filling. Check that the edges are well sealed. Cook in batches, in boiling salted water, until the ravioli float— about 4 minutes or so. Remove and set aside.

Top with your favorite pasta sauce and grated parmesan. I like Rao's sauce. To make my Nana's way, simply sauce a minced garlic clove in a big sauce pan with a teaspoon or two of olive oil. Add two cans of tomato puree and a two pound piece of chuck roast. Let the sauce simmer on low for three to four hours. Add salt and pepper to taste.